Finding Alexei
Kauai

ACI Unleashed Book 1

Olivia Sinclair

Get a free book!

Join my newsletter and get another ACI-related story available only to subscribers.

https://BookHip.com/ZNBSVAS

Prologue

Mia

I want to leap up from my uncomfortable office chair and ask my cube neighbors what they think of the job offer I'm staring at on my computer screen. The late afternoon sunlight is raking in from between the slats of the industrial blinds and casting shadows that look vaguely like prison bars across my screen.

And maybe I want to brag a little too because, well, I'm used to not being seen. Or maybe that's the wrong word. I get looked at plenty, just mostly in a way that makes me uncomfortable. As if having D cups means my brain had to sacrifice processing power in order to generate cleavage. If I remember high school biology correctly both areas require fat but completely different kinds.

Instead, I hold my excitement in (barely) even though I can feel my body quivering with repressed emotion. The office is mostly quiet. A few phone calls emanate from cubicles and the quiet hum of the copier is generating white noise down the hall.

It's that mood of being at work and not wanting to really do any work. And based on the lethargic movements of my nearest neighbors, I'd say the feeling is fairly widespread. The only thing holding me back from replying with *Yes! Yes! Yes!* to the email is the man sitting in the adjacent office. With his head held level, he's focusing on a computer screen like it holds the answers to everything in life. Alexei. He's not suffering from the late afternoon sludge. But then he never does.

He's not my boss. But he is the guy in charge of this small Sarasota office. I think it might be the smallest regional office of ACI. How Alexei ended up here nobody seems to know because he is clearly not small regional office material. He has high-ranking military written all over him. But he's really sweet. And he's looked out for me since my first day here.

When Alexei noticed how random men were stopping by my cube and leaning over the short beige walls (trying to stare down my cleavage), he asked me if it was okay if he moved me to the back corner. That way, those guys would have to walk past his office door before they got to my desk.

I said yes to that before he'd even finished his sentence. I get a lot more work done back here and the fact that when I tilt my head far enough to see over the cubicle wall, I get to see Alexei's profile isn't exactly a downside. He's gorgeous. Dark, almost black, hair that he keeps short and these mossy green eyes that make me think of ferns. And then there's that cleft in his chin. I get wet if I stare at it too long, so I try to focus on his left ear instead, which probably comes across as a little strange. Not as weird as actively panting though, so there's that.

His first name and his mother are Russian, and he got the cheekbones too. But everything else about him is pure American military. By the book, honor, integrity, and all the rest of it. What he's doing in Sarasota, I'm not entirely sure. He's not technically an office manager, even post-military. His title is something like Director of Project Operations. He spends a lot of time on his computer and he never leaves his office unattended without locking his laptop in the desk and dead-bolting the door behind him.

Which seems a bit overkill, but there are some super top secret projects in the company, so it probably has something to do with that kind of thing. And that's all I really know. Oh, and that he's forty-two, not married, and lives in a high-rise condo that he's not particularly fond of. That last little tidbit I got out of him last week when I dared ask him about his weekend when we crossed paths in the break room. I've hugged those personal little details to my heart ever since. If he knows I have a crush on him, he hasn't let on. But he's genuinely a kind man, so he probably wouldn't want to embarrass me unless he felt he had to for some reason.

I've been here almost exactly two years. I love my job, but I'm not sure Florida is for me. Not that there's anything wrong with it exactly. It's just that the cute little outfits the other women in the office wear to accommodate the heat, little business casual tanks with tiny sparkly beads and short flirty skirts, make me look like a slob. Or like I'm trying to gain the kind of attention that those idiots were offering when they kept hanging on my cube. It's a lot of work trying to find things that are suitable for the climate and still somewhat professional.

The job offer I'm still staring at is from my friend Sarah in Washington State at the Sala Bay office. I can wear sweaters again there. All year round from the sounds of things. Hearing the groan of the air conditioning kick on again as it tries to combat the sunshine sneaking in the blinds makes me salivate at the thought of cold rainy weather. It sounds absolutely delicious.

My job is mostly about sourcing fish. Sounds weird, I know. But the animal employees are a growing area of Alpha Corps' R&D department and they need to eat. And that food needs to stay fresh and also be available when they travel. So that's where I come in. Need to feed three trained sea lions for a month in Kuwait? I've got you covered — complete with the generator-powered refrigerator truck because there probably isn't a local power source close enough to the beach or dock. It's fun and challenging and I get to talk to people all over the world. I can now say 'tilapia' in ten different languages. Try bringing that out at a holiday party when you don't want to talk to someone. Works like a charm.

Sarah is a marine biologist and one of my primary human customers. We've never actually met in person, but we talk on the phone at least two or three times a week. She's a riot. And this job would be keeping my existing duties as is but adding in an additional special project working with Sarah that she just got approved. Since my technical boss is in Virginia anyway, he doesn't really care what office I work out of as long as I get the job done. It's just… Alexei. I sigh with longing and frustration. I don't want to give up on the dream, even if I know the odds are not in my favor.

If I move, I'm leaving behind any hope that he'll ever ramp up the kindness I see in his green eyes to something more. Even if it seems unlikely, a chunk of my heart keeps hoping. Because he seems lonely. He comes in early and stays late. There are no personal photos on his desk and he hasn't taken a single day of vacation while I've been here. Of course he's never said he's lonely, and he doesn't hang out and chat with people in the break room. He just… works.

I want to ask him if I should take the job, mostly to see if he has any reaction at all, but what can I say if he asks why I'm asking him? I'll blush and then if he doesn't know already he'll definitely know then how I feel about him. I need to give Sarah an answer by tomorrow, so I guess I can sleep on it and see if I have any new insights between now and then.

Leaning back in my chair, I twist my fingers through my brown curls. I wish my hair was a more exciting color. It's not horrible, it's just mid-brown. Not dark like Alexei's and nowhere close to blond. Brown. But I do have nice natural lowlights and Florida has brought out some highlights that thankfully didn't turn out to be brassy. Definitely things could be worse. My eyes scan the bland off-white ceiling tiles, hoping for inspiration when peripheral movement catches my attention. I lower my head.

That's when I spot the woman heading into Alexei's office. She's the same level of gorgeous as he is. Long dark hair hanging down her back, completely straight and thick, like a shampoo commercial. She's acting like she's trying to surprise him and it seems to work because I see him stand and look shocked. Then a delighted smile spreads across his face, into his eyes. "Nat! What are you doing here?" he asks her.

Fuck. I just got my answer, and it wasn't the one I wanted. I don't hear the rest of their conversation because somehow the tears tightening my eyes are also clogging my ears. I stare at my computer screen blindly, waiting for the dull ache to pass. I'm not jealous of that woman exactly. Oh, I could be.

I'm not denying that, but I'm so fucking envious of her ability to get that reaction from Alexei, instantly. He looked happy to see her, joyful even.

The strongest reaction I've ever gotten from him was a lot more tepid. Kind, with a huge helping of restraint. The occasional jaw tightening. I sort of had myself convinced that was who he is. Although I managed a few fantasies about how that control might play out in his bedroom. I mean, the man has to let go at some point, right?

Clearly I was wrong. Or at least deluding myself that he might pay more attention to me than the other women here. I hear the two of them leave his office after he locks up and head towards the exit. I listen to my pulse pounding in my veins until I remind myself to breathe.

Then I carefully reply to Sarah's email with an acceptance and compose a brief follow on note to my boss. I'm not losing my chance with Alexei by leaving because I never had one to begin with. That's what I need to keep reminding myself. If I keep all my attention on my job in the future, I won't be hurt like this again. That sharp stabbing feeling is just shock and disappointment. It will fade.

I

Mia

"Please, Mia? It won't be nearly as much fun without you. And you've earned the trip. Come on." Sarah is whining cheerfully while perched on the corner of my desk, her auburn hair bouncing as she does her best to convince me to come with her to Hawaii for this year's corporate war games.

"But you'll be busy with Will, and I'm not in the mood to be the sad sack of a third wheel," I pout. Sarah and her husband are the real deal, despite their twenty-year age gap. I had lunch with them once in the cafeteria, but it was clear the three or four hours they'd spent apart had been hard for both of them. They're still in the honeymoon phase and can't keep their eyes off each other. It was cute, but it made me think of Alexei. And thinking about Alexei makes me sad.

It's been nearly six months since I left the Florida office and he hasn't reached out. Not once. I didn't hold out hope that he would, which is also why I didn't go out of my way to say goodbye when I left. It felt a little desperate and I couldn't think of a casual way to mention, 'hey, I'm moving clear across the country — see you around'. I'm not even sure he knew I was leaving. He was traveling on business the day I packed up the few personal things on my desk. Sarah drags me back to the present.

"Nonsense. Just because Will and I sleep together every night doesn't mean we're not mortal enemies during working hours." She grins like she's seriously looking forward to going to battle against her husband.

"But I'm…" I gesture down at my tits.

"I know. The girls will be in good company. You've put a lot of work into this project, you should be there to help put it into action." She sits back with confidence like an attorney wrapping up closing arguments. The overhead light glints on the diamond ring she usually wears on a chain around her neck. The project she's referring to is the Triple Bs. On official paperwork it's listed as Blended Beneficial Business, but really it's the Bodacious Babes Battalion and also sometimes the Busty Bitches Brigade. Some of the guys just call it a honey trap. But HR is very clear. No sex of any kind to be offered or exchanged. But a few pouts delivered by lips dressed up in Vixen Red lipstick? Bring it on. I'm just not feeling that kind of brave right now. I'd rather the women that are get their shot at the team this year.

Sarah's having none of it. "You're going. Technically, I'm your boss for this project." She nods emphatically, and I stare at her.

"You're a year younger than I am."

"So? In this case, I know what you need. And it's not moping around this office while most of your coworkers are off frolicking in the jungles of Hawaii."

"Um, frolicking? With guns?"

"Paint ball guns. And a lot of drones. The sea lions are really looking forward to it."

"Told you that, did they?"

"Martha did. She was barking up a storm this morning. Pretty sure she's excited about the warmer water, wondering if her suit will still fit." Sarah's eyes are crinkling with laughter, but I know she actually believes those sea lions hold conversations with her. I'm not entirely sold one way or the other but they do seem to like her rather a lot… They don't spare much attention for the woman that makes sure they have fresh fish to eat. But then I'm not sure I want to be the object of sea lion affection. They are freaking *huge*.

"Okay, fine. But I am not sleeping out in a tent or whatever. I want a hotel room with a shower and air conditioning. And alcohol." I add that last inspired item, picturing myself looking out over the water at a gorgeous sunset. Alone.

"I'll see what I can do. Thank you for your service." She gives me a snappy salute and a grin before hopping down and bouncing down the corridor towards her temporary office. Her real one is at the marine center, but this project requires more central resources so she's been holed up in one of the smaller conference rooms for the last three weeks.

I sigh, thinking about flying off to a tropical island. I wanted to see Hawaii for the first time with a significant other. Romantic strolls down sandy beaches at sunset, snorkeling to see the sea turtles. It just doesn't seem like the sort of place single people go on their own. I know there must be plenty of singles living there like anywhere else in the world, but that's different. Although this is technically for work after all. And fuck, what's the weather going to be?

I quickly bring up a browser and look up Kauai in July. The internet promises warm but not extremely hot temperatures and periodic rain almost every day. It doesn't really cool down at night according to this. And of course I ditched all my Florida clothing when I got here and settled into jeans and t-shirts. With sweaters for winter. Although Sarah did say something about providing uniforms. That has me nervous because everyone on the B Brigade is a misfit in some way or another. Trying to find something that works for everyone's body type never works out on those bridal shows so why would it here? I'd better go do some quick shopping at the mall tonight.

Two weeks in Hawaii, all expenses paid. I guess I shouldn't be complaining. And at least I still haven't made it down to the shelter to adopt a cat yet. Something I've been promising myself since I gave up on love. When I get back here, I'll finally do it. And then I'll have a built in excuse the next time. I heard a rumor that for next year's games they're looking at Nevada and I hate snakes. And hot weather. And cacti.

Alexei

It's a fucking long flight from Florida to Hawaii. More like three long flights since there isn't anything direct on offer. Probably why nobody does it. Floridians head to the Keys or the Bahamas when they want a tropical island. Of course this is work, not a vacation but I'd rather be doing actual work than praying that the seat in front of me hasn't caused permanent damage to the blood flow in my legs.

The model-thin flight attendant stops by again with an offer of a tiny bag of pretzels and water. They ran out of soda, and I'm not paying for the ridiculously overpriced miniature bottles of booze. If she's lingering by my shoulder longer than other passengers' I'm not interested and I ignore her hovering presence. Instead, I lean back and close my eyes, thinking about Mia and wondering what she's up to. And whether she ran away from Florida because she read my dirty mind and wanted nothing further to do with me. I don't know if it's better or worse that I never even got the chance to kiss her before she fled.

I'm going to try to fix that error in judgment in another couple of months. If I'm not already too late. But I don't think I am. I've got contacts throughout ACI and I've been told that Mia keeps to herself and doesn't seem interested in dating her coworkers. She never did. But I thought, I hoped, she felt a little warmer towards me. There were… impediments… at the time that I'm almost done removing. And then there's the age difference. I'm too fucking old for her.

I've tried and failed to put her out of my mind several times. I'd tell her image that I was going to forget about her, not think about her anymore, and I'd manage for a few minutes. But Mia's intoxicating. And it was never even twenty-four hours before her face was swimming in front of my eyes again. Her smile warming me up from the inside. She's smart and sweet and has a body built for pleasure. It pisses me off when men sniff around her, only noticing that last one. Have the decency to ask her name before staring at her tits. On second thought, nobody gets to do that either, so just fucking stay away from her.

God, now my cock is aching. Something it does pretty much every time I take out my mental photo album of Mia. Images flash across my mind's eye.

Her gorgeous hazel eyes twinkling with laughter. Those silky sable curls I want to tangle my fingers in once I finally get to kiss her. That time I saw her bent over the front of her car, trying to figure out why it wouldn't start. I fixed that for her *after* I had myself back under control. The curve of her ass is perfection. And the way she bites the corner of her lip when she's nervous and trying to choose her words carefully. Something I wish she didn't feel like she has to do around me.

Just a couple more signatures on some pieces of paper and I can be blunt with her. Well, straight up about the personal stuff. The classified information will have to stay that way. But by then I won't have to think about those things either, so we should be fine. Which is good because once I get a taste of her, I'm not sure I'm ever going to be able to walk away. My eyes might be open again, staring at the royal blue upholstery of the seat in front of me, but all I'm really seeing is Mia.

When the plane finally touches down in Hawaii, the long day plus the time change has my body wanting nothing more than a stiff drink and a bed. I'm beyond pissed when I realize ACI has decided to save money by having everyone bunk at the site rather than at a hotel for the two days before the events officially kickoff. So after a bumpy ride on an old school bus, I'm staring down at the military canvas cot lined up with twenty others in a row.

I'm thrown back to my boot camp days. Fuck it. I'm too tired to argue with anyone about the sleeping arrangements. Some guy offers me a bottle of vodka with a silently raised eyebrow, and I nod with relief. He hands me a plastic glass half full, as if knowing words aren't going to make anything better.

I down the liquor and hit the shower before lying face down on the damn cot. I'm too old for this shit. Fifteen days more of this and I can get on with my life. I ignore the low rumble of men talking — reuniting with old buddies and acquaintances. Bringing old service rivalries back to life. I've been there, done that at these things in the past.

In the morning, over breakfast in a large tent serving as the mess hall for this quadrant, I get my assignment for the games. I'm to be the operational perimeter guard for one of the back roads. I grunt, accepting it with an internal eye roll. It's good and bad and somewhat of an acknowledgment of my age and experience. As in they know I don't really want to be here. And since I was (and am) in a very secret branch of special ops for almost my entire military career I'm not part of the two major combatants this year which is Army vs Navy. The good news is I don't have to wander around in the jungle, slipping and sliding in the red mud. The downside is I can't get 'killed' either, which would put me back in a real hotel a few days faster. I'm stuck in my temporary duty hut from 8 am to 6 pm unless relieved for meals or some kind of meeting. Aside from a handful of newbies, most of the guys plus the handful of women that are here know how to stay within the defined perimeter of the event. So while I'll mostly be bored, if I am needed it will be important. Or so the little slip of paper I've been handed states. I'm not convinced. But I'm also not looking for one more challenge on my plate at the moment either. I sigh and slip the paper into my pocket. I'm not expected to report to my hut until tomorrow, so there's that.

Damn good thing I've got a few books loaded up on my phone. Mia was always sneaking romances over her lunch break, even though she thought nobody noticed. So I've stalked some of her social media profiles to figure out what she likes. Laugh all you want, basic intel like this can make the difference in a hearts and minds campaign. I just have to decide if I'm brave enough to start with *The Virgin's Second Chance* or not. She seemed to really like it based on the review she posted. Ever since I found that I've been wondering if Mia is still a virgin. It wouldn't change my opinion of her but I might have to alter a few plans, go a little slower on the flinging her over my shoulder part. She's still ending up in my bed for the rest of her life, if I have anything to say about it.

2

★ ★ ★

Mia

I look around the relatively small olive green tent (it's small only in comparison to the others really) and wonder if this is what boarding school is like. Five other women are giggling and chattering in between sips of coffee from white paper cups as they get ready for our first day as official war games vamps. The uniform we were all handed is a black wrap dress. They're sized so you can choose from almost nothing showing to down-to-the-navel cleavage with a sleeveless or fluttery sleeve option.

There's also deep rich red lipstick and matching nail polish. The overall image is somewhat ruined by the footwear which are black hiking shoes. Even worse is the required lanyard with an attached badge that has our name and classification written out across the back. Just in case, I guess. The shoes are required by health and safety because it rains at some point almost every day and the ground can get slippery and muddy.

Sarah and I both frowned over this unfortunate news but had to acknowledge that spies with broken ankles weren't going to help our cause any, so we didn't put up a fight. We just pouted over the impact on the overall look and resolved to find cuter shoes that met the safety requirements for next year. Assuming we get to do this again.

The higher-ups are so nervous about this whole flirting initiative that we're stationed in smaller tents on the completely other side of the compound from the guys. Mind you, the women who have served in the military get their tents right next to the big barracks ones for the men. That doesn't make any sense to me, but so many things don't.

So here we are in groups of six, there are twenty-five of us in total, but Sarah made it clear she was with Will every night and that was non-negotiable. She won't tell me why it's so important, but I'm sure it's not just pure lust. She gets this little quiver at the corner of her lips whenever it comes up, so I know it's something that makes her laugh.

The air here smells different from the mainland. It's not just because it's warm and humid but I can't quite put my finger on it either. I'm looking forward to seeing more of Hawaii outside this tent. We arrived late last night, so I didn't get to see much coming in, but I'm hoping to visit one of the bamboo forests I've heard so much about. I don't want to get lost in one though.

For luck I'm wearing my absolute favorite bra and panty set. It's hot pink with metallic gold embroidery. Way too flashy to ever wear to work, even under my clothes, because if anyone ever caught a glimpse of it… But here, with almost total strangers and under the black dress, they're perfect. And I feel exotic and ready to spy on a military installation. Sort of.

I gather what I need for the day and head to the small mess tent. Since it's just us on this side of the compound, we only get coffee and a Continental style breakfast, but at least there's fresh pineapple and mango along with some basic pastries. I'm too nervous about our first day of spying to eat much, but I'm already wondering how we're supposed to find lunch. Probably not a good sign of my future in espionage!

After breakfast, which goes by way too fast, a bus shows up to take us over to the other side. There's going to be an official briefing before everyone is ferried to their individual start points. A lot of money and planning has gone into this thing. I really had no idea it was such a big deal, even though I've been working with Sarah on it for the last several months. Numbers on a page are just different from seeing it all laid out in real life.

The massive tent they have set up has full audio and visual and even a small stage. The content though is boring as hell. The scenario being played out is something about claiming ownership of some fictional mines in the jungle that give something or other important for maintaining peace and security. I've no idea if that's real or made up because I've never heard of that mineral compound before.

The rest of the speech goes by in a flurry of military acronyms and buzzwords that I don't even try to follow. Mostly I look around and marvel at the sheer number of good-looking men getting ready to play in the mud.

Finally my name is called and I'm handed a small folder with my individual assignment. I'm to assess the northern perimeter and gather any intelligence I can about access and troop movements from the entry points in that sector. Sounds easy enough if only I knew where the northern perimeter was. I also have to be careful not to be hit by a paintball gun as then I will be 'dead' and have to spend the rest of the two weeks arranging chairs in the big tent. That was Sarah's threat, that she added as she pointed me to the right bus to go to my station. She seemed excited about something, but she got called away before I could ask her about it.

Anyone could be forgiven for thinking the bus was full of noisy school kids. People are laughing and joking, smack talking back and forth. Gradually it empties of occupants until there are only a couple of us left. I eye the verdant landscape out the window. It all looks so foreign, even though Florida was tropical too. The air is heavy and humid, making it almost hard to breathe. The bus groans to a halt with screechy brakes. "Milepost 67," the driver calls out. That's my stop. I grab my tote bag that has my water bottle and sunscreen, along with my map and compass, and make my way to the front. As soon as both feet are on the dusty red ground, the bus pulls away. I'm left staring after it because there is nothing but road and greenery in every possible direction. Where am I supposed to go from here again?

I check my instructions and the small map several times. I'm supposed to walk about a quarter of a mile and then there should be another road where I turn right. Anything after that intersection is my assigned territory for intel and as of now I'm a potential target for assassination. Oh goody.

I look furtively around to see if there are any guns pointed at me from the depths of the jungle. Nothing that I can see, but then it should be fairly obvious I'm no good at this sort of thing. I'll be embarrassed if I'm killed before the end of the first day, though. I decide my top priority is to get off this main road. And while it might be entertaining to walk through the underbrush, I'll make faster time if I stick to the track. I pick up my pace.

When I spot dust kicking up in the distance, I duck behind something that looks like a philodendron on speed until I see the small car pass. It doesn't look like it has anything to do with the war games, but appearances can be deceiving. I wait, admiring a colorful bug crawling along a leaf until I'm sure the occupants of the car won't be able to see me in their rear-view mirror.

After about ten minutes of walking, I come up to the intersection. And that's when the wind starts blowing through the tops of the palm trees and other tall vegetation. Nothing's coming out of the sky, but I eye it with misgiving because everything in me says a storm is brewing. I turn around, and the sky behind me has gone eerily black. There's still plenty of light but… I walk faster because even though I don't know what I'm looking for, I'm hoping to find something that will serve as better shelter.

Rain pings out of the sky with enough velocity to actually sting where it hits my bare skin. The weird thing is it's warm. I'm so used to rain being colder than the surrounding air, even with a midsummer thunderstorm, that this feels weird. I'd enjoy it more if I wasn't out here in the wilderness by myself. The air has a slightly metallic taste that has my nerves on edge.

Finally I see a slight glint of metal up ahead. Not soon enough, really, because I'm drenched already. My hair is flattened against my face, water dripping from the ends, adding to the raindrops hitting it. And my dress, looking so sexy just an hour ago, is a sodden mess clinging to me everywhere and making it hard to move. I waddle towards the metal corrugated roof. Even if it's some kind of rough barn,

I need shelter before I drown out here.

The roof resolves itself into a small hut-like thing. It has two open sides so no need for a door but it looks fairly dry as the roof is slanted away from the prevailing winds. Which thankfully this sudden storm is adhering to. And as I mentioned, at least I'm not cold. Not yet. I've no idea how I'm supposed to make it back to base. I doubt the bus will be swinging back in this. Besides, the bus was supposedly a onetime deal to get everyone into position quickly. You're supposed to be able to make your own way back. Damn these military survivalists.

As soon as I'm sufficiently under the roof to not feel rain on my face, I wrestle with the wet blanket that used to be my dress until I finally get it off. I'm wringing it out as best I can when I hear a muffled choking sound followed by, "Mia, is that you?"

3

★　★　★

Mia

Oh my God. There's someone here. I freeze, looking furtively around without turning my head, but I can't see anyone. The sky has darkened considerably as the rain pours down and even though the space isn't big, it's mostly dark shadows. I squint, trying to see into the corners.

And I'm as good as naked. Worse, whoever it is, is getting an up close and personal view of my hot pink underwear. I clutch the sodden mass of my dress to my chest and turn in a circle slowly. Deep in the shadows, leaning against the far wall, is a man. My heart stops. Why has he been so quiet? And why am I not more scared? I could be murdered out here and nobody would ever find me. But there's something about his stance that seems familiar. Then the man moves slightly and I know.

"Alexei?" My voice squeaks in horror.

His lips twitch slightly, but his expression isn't amused. It's fierce and predatory. In an instant, he's up and taking my dress from my hands. He tosses it onto a small shelf attached to the wall before pulling me by my upper arms until I'm standing up straight. I can't cover myself, his firm grip on my biceps has my hands flopping at my sides. And maybe I don't want to. The heat in his gaze as it sweeps over me is enough to light a fire under just about anything.

"What are you doing here?" I finally get out before gulping.

"I could ask you the same thing." He nods in the direction of the badge on the lanyard that's still around my neck. "What's that all about, then? The Vixen Brigade?"

"Oh, um. I'm a spy of sorts. We seductively obtain information."

"The hell you do. That stops now." His voice is sharp and his hands tighten reflexively. I'm going to wake up to bruises on my arms. How am I going to explain that to my tent mates?

"Alexei. Let go of me, it's okay. It's all HR approved. Well, I'm not saying they approve so much as they couldn't find a reason why we couldn't do it."

"Well, I can," he growls. For some reason, that dent in his chin is looking extra delectable.

"Are you going to shoot me?" I ask tentatively. I don't want to be shot by a paintball gun while wearing nothing but my bra and panties, but if it's going to happen, I'd rather it was Alexei doing it.

"What?" He looks horrified and then I think the light bulb goes off. "Oh. That. No, I'm here for perimeter control. Make sure nothing here spills over into civilian territory or vice versa."

I sag with relief. "Oh good. That would be embarrassing."

His left eyebrow quirks as if it to inquire how my current situation is escaping that fate, but I ignore it.

"Mia," he groans, and I wait for him to finish what he's saying, but he doesn't utter another word. He just picks me up like I weigh nothing at all and carries me over to a bar stool, apparently the only furniture in the place. He sets me down and then grabs a small towel out of a bag and begins to tenderly wipe the rain off my face.

"I'm afraid I only have the one towel so it won't be enough for your hair," he finally comments.

"Errr. My dress…"

"Is wet and heavy. You're fine as you are for the moment. We aren't likely to get company any time soon."

I can feel the blush heating my cheeks as I duck my head. I can't look at him. This is so embarrassing. What the hell must he think of me now? I try to breathe slowly and deeply, but that makes me inhale his scent and my entire body reacts. He smells like the ocean, refreshing and slightly salty. I want to lick him to see if he tastes the same way.

Alexei's wearing an ugly orange Hawaiian-print shirt, one that I now recognize as marking an official — neutral as to the two sides but also in authority over both.

"Mia?"

I shake my head, still not willing to look at him, and I hear him snort softly. His hands are now running up and down my arms gently. "Mia? Did I do or say anything to make you leave Florida so abruptly?"

"What? No!" I glance up at his question because I'm so surprised. I don't expect the stern grooves that have formed along his mouth, and I pull back slightly.

"Then why did you leave?"

"Um, well." I hurriedly try to think of a reason that won't expose my crush on him. "I got a job offer."

"And you couldn't say goodbye?"

"You seemed busy. I didn't want to impose." I twist my fingers together, hoping he'll drop the subject soon.

"How about you try the actual story now because you're a terrible liar." He says it almost fondly, like he's glad about that.

I try my trick of looking at his left ear, but it's not

working this time. His body is radiating heat and there's something about the steamy air around us that has me feeling completely natural being mostly naked. And that makes me think of *other* natural things to do while naked. My nipples are rigid against the lace embroidery of my bra, the wet fabric abrading them in a special kind of torture. I arch my back instinctively, but that pushes my chest against his and I jerk back.

"I uh, there was a man." His fingers tense on my arms again while he waits for me to speak. "He… I… he wasn't interested. And I wanted to get away."

There's a long, painful silence. I watch the pulse in his jaw throb, one… two… three…

"Are you still in love with him?" Alexei finally growls.

"I… I've decided to focus on my job."

"That doesn't answer my question."

I shrug. "It's the best I've got," I answer defiantly, meeting his eyes for the first time since he went down this line of questioning.

His lips quirk at the corners slightly when I say that. I hold my breath, wondering if my half-truth is enough to distract him. I will die if I have to confess my crush on this gorgeous man while wearing hot pink and gold underwear and nothing else. Well, I do still have my hiking shoes on, but that somehow only makes things worse.

Alexei

Without warning, this annoying assignment just got a lot more interesting. But it's taking everything in me not to press Mia up against the rickety wall and physically convince her that I'm the only man she should be looking at. How can I have missed that she was sighing over another man while I was watching her, fantasizing about our future together? And who the hell is he?

I'd have noticed if anyone has stopped by her cubicle frequently. I made sure nobody was hassling her if it wasn't work related and she's too damn good at her job to get much of that. She did say he wasn't that in to her, which is impossible to believe. What straight man would turn her down? What man of any sexual orientation wouldn't follow her around the planet just to be the recipient of her glowing smile? The one that makes you feel like you're the only man she sees?

Some kind of sensory sixth sense pulses through my bloodstream. Mia smiled at me like that. Back in Florida. Her eyes dewy soft and those plump lips curved up hopefully as she tried to get more than one-word answers out of me with teasing questions. I admit I kept things short just to watch her try to pull more out of me. It was my one indulgence since I couldn't do what I wanted to most.

She wasn't meeting my eyes when she confessed her reason for leaving Florida a few minutes ago. Is it simply my hopeful ego thinking she was trying to talk around an attraction to me? Despite her denial, am I the real reason she left? I eye her speculatively. She's still not looking at me directly. Her gaze focused on the rain coming down in torrents outside the small shelter and running off the corrugated metal of the roof. I'm thankful it's not cold. Or then again, if it was, I'd have a ready excuse for wrapping her tight against me.

Mia's skin glows in the moisture laden air. She's fucking beautiful. My eyes drink her in because it's been so damn long since they've feasted. But I have to know what I'm up against. "Mia? Tell me about this guy that wasn't into you because I find that almost impossible to believe."

"You do?" she half-croaks, her eyes widening with panic. My heart picks up another beat. I nod.

"Why?" she asks breathlessly.

"Because you're perfect."

"Nooo... I'm definitely not that." She half laughs, her eyes casting around wildly for something to look at that isn't me. I place my index finger under her chin and guide her face back towards mine.

"Mia. I'll know if you lie. And there will be consequences this time."

"There will?" She visibly gulps, and I have to bite back my smile. I think she just gave the whole thing away because she leaned forward when I said that. And I've learned something new that we might have to investigate later. Together. I think my sweet girl might like being bossed around in bed.

I nod firmly, my eyes holding hers, not letting her look away. "Was it me, Mia? Did you leave because of me?"

I don't know what I was expecting, but it sure as hell wasn't the silent tears that start spilling down her cheeks. Fuck. I pull her tight against me, my hands splayed across the warm skin of her back. "I know I'm not the most sociable guy but tears, Mia? Am I that bad?"

She mumbles something against my chest while my fingers tangle in her thick hair. Her curls are even softer than I'd imagined. I loosen my grip but she doesn't pull back, just burrows deeper against me. I close my arms again. Holding her tight. "Sweetheart? I couldn't make that out. Say it again?"

She shifts her head to the side, facing away from me. "You were plenty sociable for your girlfriend."

My jaw is hanging open. "What girlfriend? I haven't been with a woman in over three years. I've been fucking waiting to get my hands on you, Mia."

"She came to visit you. You smiled at her. You never smiled at me like that." The tears are flowing again, splatting against my arm that I refuse to move despite Mia trying to push me away. With my luck I'd have to chase her out into the monsoon we seem to be experiencing.

I think back to who the hell she could be talking about. Some woman that came to see me? I can't think of anyone that wasn't already working in my office stopping by. Except my cousin... "Hell, are you talking about my cousin, Natalia?"

Mia shrugs against my arms, but doesn't say anything. "My first cousin. Just so we're clear." I tell her dryly. Fuck, have we wasted the last six months because she thought...

"Doesn't matter." Mia states more firmly, her head no longer resting on my arm. "You smiled like you were genuinely happy. That made it obvious that you didn't feel that way about me. Not that I had any right to expect that you would. I just didn't need to be reminded of that every day."

Ah, hell. I look around this miserable little hut frantically. There's really nowhere comfortable to sit. The ground it is. I tug Mia over to the driest corner and slide down the support beam, taking her into my arms so she's stretched out over me. Every part of her is stiff.

"Mia. Look at me." I inject my voice with as much

commanding force as I dare, leaving it just short of a bark. She flinches, but eventually raises her eyes to mine.

"Have you ever wanted something so badly your heart hurt just thinking about it?" My arms are locked around her, she's not going anywhere until we have this out.

"Um. No? I'm not sure. My heart isn't feeling all that great at the moment," she says wryly.

I drop a swift kiss on the top of her head in sympathy. "You're it for me, Mia. It's been killing me that I couldn't take you in my arms and show you how you make me feel. There were… reasons I couldn't do that at the time. Fuck, there are reasons I shouldn't be doing this now, but to hell with it. I'm not letting you go."

She blinks slowly. "I'm confused."

I nod in response. "I know. I'm sorry. I can't tell you all of it. But I promise you the only reason I ever had not to smile was because my cock was too desperate to sink into you. *Is* desperate," I amend, giving her a small glare.

Mia's face is skeptical. I shift her on my lap until my cock is pressing up against the thin fabric of her panties, right up against her luscious folds. She gulps, her eyes swallowing her face. "Alexei?"

"Kitten."

She shifts her sweet center, grinding down on me ever so slightly, then biting her plump lower lip. "Why didn't you say anything?"

I sigh, I wonder that myself, in hindsight. "I thought I had more time to ease you into the idea. And I was hoping to wrap up a few obligations, so that I was free to pursue a future with you without interruptions. I've been doing that anyway. Another couple of weeks and you will have my undivided attention."

She still looks uncertain, her delicate eyebrows drawn in towards her nose in concentration. She's absolutely adorable.

4

★ ★ ★

Mia

I shift anxiously while perching on Alexei's lap. His doing, not mine. I don't know this Alexei. He's not the kind, gentle giant I thought I knew. This man is fierce… and hard. His thick cock is pressing insistently against me through the fabric of his pants, even though he's not moving a millimeter. My pussy aches to enfold him, take him inside of me, and forget everything else. But my brain won't let me. I need to take this slowly because I feel like I'm missing something. Something so obvious I should know it already.

Frowning, I stare down at my hands spread across the god-awful orange of his shirt. It clashes hideously with my pink underwear. I giggle, and Alexei quirks an eyebrow at me. "We're quite the fashionable pair," I whisper.

"You're beautiful, kitten." His hands clench into the flesh of my thighs with authority. Like he's going to punish me if I disagree with him. Where did that thought come from? And why did it send a wave of wetness into my panties? I shift again, trying to find a way to sit here that doesn't have me rubbing up against him like a bitch in heat. But Alexei tightens his hands again, holding me in place with his cock throbbing against my pussy, and I decide to let it all be. For the moment, anyway.

"I... what do we do now?" I ask almost plaintively. I don't have a plan for this scenario.

I'm not sure Alexei does either, but he surprises me. "First, we wait for the rain to calm down. Then we head back to central command where you will be unassigned from this damn vixen thing. Then we're going to go eat somewhere that does not involve a tent followed by sleeping that doesn't either. I'm not letting you out of my sight so resign yourself now to sleeping wrapped in my arms." He's practically growling as his green eyes stare me down with challenge. I gulp.

"Ummm. What if I want to be a Vixen?"

"Kitten, you can interrogate me all you want but you are not flashing those pretty eyes of yours at any other man."

I pout. It's not that I'm really excited to go out flirting, but I was hoping to gain some confidence from this whole exercise. Confidence I'm clearly going to need to deal with this man. The one who's been hiding inside the reserved Alexei I thought I knew.

"Mia? I mean it. You're done."

"But… I want to see if I can do it."

"Then practice on me."

"It's not the same."

"Why not?" Alexei pulls me tighter against his chest.

"Because you're not on the fighting forces. I'm supposed to gather intel from them."

"Why wouldn't they just shoot you with one of the paint guns?"

"Because that would be rude?"

"Mia." His tone of disbelief has me giggling.

"I'm too wet to do anything about it now, anyway. But *I* will decide in the morning. Me. Not you, tough guy."

"You're wet?" His green eyes smolder with fire, his hand shifting around to nudge up against my pussy. I moan as his fingers brush the soft skin of my inner thigh.

"Not what I meant. Rain." I can't talk. His thick fingers are stroking me softly over the fabric of my panties. "But you are wet, aren't you, kitten? This isn't water from the sky." He brings his finger up to his lips and flicks out his tongue. "Sweet."

I gape at him, shocked by his actions. His eyes soften. That kindness I'm more familiar with making a brief appearance.

"Mia? Baby. I need you to tell me why that shocked you. How much experience have you had?"

I resort to staring at his ear again and bite my lip, unsure how to answer that. Or why I need to. I glance down, seeing the way my nipples are hard and pressing against the lace of my bra. I frown.

"Kitten, we're going to end up in exactly the same place, regardless. You can't push me away no matter what you say. But you need to tell me."

I shake my head no. I really don't.

"Okay. Let me show you how interrogation works when done correctly." Alexei wraps one arm more firmly around my waist and reaches for my hiking boots with the other. A few undone laces and a yank or two, and his thick fingers are sliding erotically between my toes. He pushes them back and forth, catching those hidden corners full of nerve endings until my toes are curling and my back is arching with need. Fuck.

"Are you a virgin, Mia?" he asks softly, biting down gently on my earlobe. I can feel the flush spreading over my entire body. "Hmmm," he hums approvingly. "Have you even kissed a man before?" This at least I've done, and I notice his mouth tighten at the corners. "Ever sucked a man's cock between those pink lips, baby?" This time I shake my head. My eyes glued to his. "What about a man kissing that sweet virgin pussy?" I blush harder. I don't want to think about *that*. Not with Alexei's cock pushing angrily against my thigh. It's too much.

"Good girl." He presses a soft kiss to the side of my neck. Probably because I'm now hiding my face against his shoulder. "See? That wasn't so bad, was it?" He leans down and gives me a patronizing kiss on the top of my head. I know he's doing that to be an ass, to relieve me of my embarrassment, and I feel my eyes filling back up with tears because he's so unbearably sweet. While being annoyingly bossy as fuck.

Alexei

Holding Mia like this makes me never want to let go. She's both everything and more than I ever imagined. Better than in my dreams. She's the perfect armful and so fucking *soft*. No way in hell am I letting her go out there to try to coax information out of a bunch of seasoned military guys. They'll eat Mia alive. She has no idea how charming and sweet she is or just how far a man will go to get a taste of that. I know what I'd do to get her to look at me twice and I'm not going to give another guy that kind of chance.

Right now I think she's doing her best to pretend I'm not even here. Kinda difficult when parts of me are hard enough to bend steel. Not to mention poking at her softness like the sun rising in the morning depends on me fucking her at the earliest opportunity. But she's giving it everything she has to ignore all that, keeping her beautiful face hidden against my shoulder and barely moving. I'd happily stay here for eternity just holding her, but eventually we're going to need to eat. Not to mention if it keeps raining like this, the flimsy hut is going to eventually succumb to all the water.

I shift Mia ever so slightly on my lap so I can reach into my pocket for my phone. There's supposed to be some kind of alert for bad weather or other major events, but apparently I have no signal out here. Great. I lean my head back against the post and try to think.

But when I do that, there's a vibration in the wood strong enough to catch my attention. Something big is headed this way. "Mia, baby? Stop playing possum. I think something's on its way to pick us up."

She leans her head back, her eyes frantic, darting around the hut before landing on her still dripping dress.

"Here. Sit up for a minute. You can have my shirt."

"But…"

"Have I given you any indication that I'd be okay with random strangers seeing you in your underwear?" I ask dryly.

"Um, no? But…"

I hurriedly undo the five or six buttons down the front and slip it off my shoulders and over Mia's. She bats my hands away when I go to button it and does it herself. She's still frowning down at the shirt. I mean, I know it's not the greatest fashion but…

"It's way too short to cover my ass."

Fuck. "Stand up and let's see." I shift her off of me as gently as I can so I can jump up and pull her upright. She's not wrong. The end of the shirt leaves a tantalizing peek-a-boo of hot pink front and back. If we weren't about to have company, I would absolutely take my time to savor it. A loud clanging bang and a squeal of brakes announce something big pulling up outside. "Just stay behind me as best you can," I tell her.

There's a funky jeep thing sitting just in front of the hut. Mia is frozen where she stands, staring at my chest. "Mia?"

"Hmmm?" She's responding, but not looking at me. Or rather she is looking at me, but not my face. If I had any doubts left that she has feelings for me, they're gone now. "Mia, it's time to go. Hold that thought for another twenty or thirty minutes."

She blushes hard and hot, but finally shifts her eyes to the man getting out of the vehicle. He's looking worried. "You Mia Tennant?" he asks her.

She nods.

"Thank fuck for that." He gestures both of us to the back of the vehicle. I'm frowning at his cavalier attitude. But a ride is a ride. I calm down a little when he starts down the road again. "I'm Mike. Everyone else is accounted for, but neither of you were responding to calls. Ms. Tennant here was not where she was expected to be. Thought I was going to have to fill out a mile of paperwork and launch search and rescue." He rubs a big hand through his sandy hair before looking in the rear-view mirror at Mia. "You alright there, Miss? We'll be back at HQ in a jiffy."

Mia just nods and tugs on the shirt hem, trying to stretch it out to cover her generous assets. I put my hand over hers to still her movements. No need to call attention to what we can't do anything about. She bites her lip and looks down at our clasped hands. And heaves a big sigh.

"Is there food there?" she finally asks.

"Not sure. That was the original plan, but this storm caught everyone by surprise. They'll come up with something," Mike responds cheerfully, navigating around a small lake that's appeared in the middle of the muddy red road. It's a bumpy ride and if that has Mia bouncing her tits against my side, more than would happen in a city, well, thank fuck for small blessings.

5

★　★　★

Mia

Right now the world bears very little resemblance to the one I woke up to this morning. On the con side, there's the whole wandering around Hawaii half naked and not in a good way. Why did I put on the hot pink undies again? Admittedly, I didn't expect to be flashing the entire island, but half the world's mothers are constantly warning their children about the risks of leaving the house without clean underwear. Including my own. They were clean by the way but I think we can take that homily as implied to extend to 'don't wear overly eye-catching underwear either'.

But then on the pro side of the equation there's Alexei. Who not only has appeared back in my life out of nowhere but has gone from the rather stern teddy bear I remember sighing over into what I can only describe as a hot-as-fuck possessive alpha male. Who wants to fuck *me*? I'm still trying to wrap my head around that one. Yes, I fantasized about exactly that scenario, but it's no different from a teenage girl dreaming about her favorite rock star. She'd be pretty damn shocked if he showed up at her birthday party.

And as delicious as the thought of being claimed by Alexei is, it's becoming clear that I'm going to have to enforce a certain amount of independence. Or he's going to having me caving with the slightest quirk of his eyebrow. I came here to do a job and I'm determined to do it to the best of my abilities. Never mind that I told Sarah I didn't want to come. And Alexei's sexy growls in my ear about how I should never be looked at by another man are nice but not practical. I know he doesn't literally want to lock me away. I think.

I'm still not convinced that he'll want me once he really gets to know me. I mean, I'm pretty ordinary outside of my job coordinating fish deliveries, which if you take away the fish part is a straightforward mid-level purchasing and logistics job. I've never even had what I would call a real boyfriend. Don't you have to get past three dates for that? And none of the dates I've ever been on were memorable enough to make me feel like I was missing something.

There's no doubt in my mind that a night (heck, an hour) in Alexei's bed would be something I would never forget or regret. I'd haul him down in the back of this jeep if I thought I could ever offer the same to him. I'm afraid I'm utterly forgettable. It's never really bothered me before, well, except for where Alexei is concerned, but we've been over that.

Now he's looking at me like the sea lions stare at Sarah when she's holding the last fish and they know if they take their eyes off it, one of the others will gobble it right up. See? I can't even describe a man's lust-filled eyes without bringing fish into it. How sexy is that? God help me.

The jeep thing grinds to a clanking halt in front of a large, very wet-looking tent. Alexei bends down to whisper in my ear, "Wait here, I'll go find something for you to wear." Then he raises his voice to carry over the rain pinging on the metal roof to Mike. "I'll be back in a sec, don't want Mia getting any wetter than necessary."

Mike looks at me in the rear-view mirror with a puzzled expression, but nods once and leans back. Alexei opens the door and dashes for the tent, his shoulders military level, not moving an iota. It's a long, tense few moments until he comes back with a dark bundle in his arms. He leans in and tosses the fabric to me. It's an odd-looking duster coat of waxed cotton. I'm not sure how much water it's going to keep off, but it will cover me and I'm beyond grateful. I tug it on, trying not to flash Mike any more than necessary and belt it tightly. Then I'm sliding over the bench seat and Alexei is helping me out. Together this time, we dash for cover.

Right away, Sarah is pulling me into her arms. "Fuck, Mia. I was so worried about you. I'm glad to see you're okay." She tries to lead me over to some chairs by one of those industrial plastic coffee dispensers, but there's a dead weight attached to my other arm. I look over my shoulder to see Alexei rooted in place, his large hand clasped around my hand *and* my wrist. Sarah turns too, probably to see what the holdup is. I hear a soft snort laugh from her direction, but she stops pulling on my arm. "What?" I'm not entirely sure why he doesn't want me getting coffee. It's not like I'll be out of his sight.

"We aren't done with our earlier conversation, Mia. We clear on that?" His voice is stern and everything about him is tense.

My jaw drops and I half nod. "Um, okay?" I'm really not sure what he's getting at.

He sighs and relaxes half a notch. "Do not leave this tent without letting me know or when I find you, I'll be making you very sorry."

I blush, my entire body hot with need. It's not that I'm that turned on by the thought of whatever it is he's threatening, it's the vision of winding Alexei up enough for him to even think of it. Sarah groans behind me, "Where did you find him?"

Alexei lets go of my hand with a curt nod and I go off numbly with Sarah for a different type of interrogation.

Alexei

"*That's* Alexei?" an astonished voice rises above the din in the tent and I glance over to see it's coming from the woman with Mia. My girl blushes slightly and casts a worried look my way to see if I heard that. I smirk in response and she turns back, her cheeks even redder than before. I want to throw her over my shoulder and go find a hotel room where I can fuck her until she finally understands how irresistible she is. Then I can't wait to hear what she's been telling her friends about me, so I can tease her until she blushes. But I know it's going to have to wait a few more hours. I'm not going to be patient any longer than that, though. Those days are over.

Mia has her head close to the other woman's, they're chattering and gesticulating like they haven't seen each other in years but I'm pretty sure that's the woman trying to send Mia out to seduce guys. I glare at the thought and the young woman looks up right then and just rolls her eyes. An older, former military man comes up behind her and kisses her neck discretely. If I hadn't been watching the two of them like a hawk, I wouldn't have noticed. She softens instantly and I revise my opinion of her. Up to a point. My Mia is not seducing anyone but me. Just so we're clear.

I could stand here staring at Mia all day, but I suppose I should take care of some business, so I'm free to spend the evening with her without arguing with management. I scan the tent, looking for a recognizable face with some influence over this shit fest. Ah. Just the man. Lukas is attempting to take a nap while sitting up in the far corner deep in the shadows. I make a beeline over there and jam his cap down over his eyes. He surges up, fists raised, until he sees me. Then he relaxes with a big shit-eating grin. "Alexei, should have known they'd let the trash in on this one." That insult is followed by one of those manly handshakes that's really arm wrestling without a table. Naturally I win and he's stuck wringing his hand out, trying to get the blood flowing again.

"What do you want, Alexei?"

"Intel. And a change of assignment. Turns out my girl is here and some idiot wants her out seducing other men."

He sighs heavily, like he's heard this a thousand times already. "They're not seducing anyone, not physically anyway. It's all psychological and management wants it in place. This year is the trial run. They want to see what weaknesses it exposes and also tap any potential female leadership so their diversity numbers look better."

"Fuck that shit."

Lukas rolls his eyes. "Same crap everywhere, Alexei. Get over it."

"I don't give a damn about any of the others, but

Mia is not rolling those big eyes at anyone else. Who do I have to kill to make that happen?"

"Prison isn't going to help keep your girl away from other men, hotshot. No killing. No hitting. Got it?"

He's right and I know it, but my inner six-year-old is having a hard time backing down from the playground fight. I've waited so fucking long to hold Mia. These last few hours are the hardest yet. "Back to my question. I want her off this squad and I intend to be glued to her side for the remainder of this cluster fuck so make it happen."

He blinks at me. "Not my commanding officer, Alexei, or my boss or anything but an old friend, and I didn't hear the magic word." He's teasing now, and it's annoying as fuck.

"Please," I grate out through clenched teeth.

"There, was that so hard? If you agree that I am a vastly superior being, more intelligent, better looking, and charming beyond belief I think I can make something work in your favor."

"Lukas," I warn, dangerously close to the edge. He's a good friend normally, but he's tap dancing on my last nerve and he knows it.

Finally he relents. "There's a nice little cruiser moored at the dock in the southeast quadrant. Needs perimeter control same as the road checkpoints. I can also move your girl there under the theory that any incoming from either side could be possible targets for questioning."

"So I'd be there with her?"

"The whole time. Boat's too small for too many visitors, so I'm guessing any conversations would be held over open water. And there's a small berth down below not that I'm suggesting you sleep on the job or anything."

I glare at him. I don't know where this completely possessive streak came from, but I'm ready to tear into him for even the suggestion of Mia naked. I can't say that he even knows what she looks like, so I don't think he's doing anything deliberately offensive.

"Thanks, man." I give way grudgingly.

"Invite me to the wedding." Lukas grins. "You've got it bad."

I nod jerkily. I do. "So about tonight, is there a fucking real hotel around here?"

His grin widens. "Can't wait for the romance of a boat, huh? There's a couple of B&B's up the main road and one of those eco resorts if you leave the compound going the other way. Can't imagine there're any vacancies though, not with this weather."

I grunt at that assessment and scan the crowd again, looking to see if there's anyone with better connections into the local area. Razz was from Hawaii originally, wasn't he? I wander over his direction and nod when he meets my gaze. "You know this area?"

He shrugs. "Not my hometown, but I have some family nearby. Why?"

"Need a nicer place to stay tonight. My girl's in town."

There's no mistaking the twinkle that appears in his eyes. "Finally fell, tough guy? Must hurt after all these years."

"You have no fucking idea," I acknowledge with chagrin.

"Just so happens I think I can fix you up. My cousin has a small vacation place here, it's a little further out so I haven't bothered because it's more fun to hang with the guys. But it's your lucky day if you don't mind a drive."

"The further away from this mess the better."

He digs in his pocket and dangles a key in front of me. I snatch it before he can change his mind. "You'll need to stop at the corner store for food, and they only stock local eats, plenty of canned ham, none of your fancy mainland crap."

I nod. I don't give a damn about food beyond making sure Mia isn't starving. Razz rattles off basic directions and how to know we're at the right place. I memorize it all and turn to find Mia. That's when I realize she's no longer in the tent. Fuck it all.

6

★ ★ ★

Mia

Sarah is still chattering in my ear, updating me on what all the other girls have accomplished with the day (hint, it's a lot more than me) as she gently drags me from the tent. I look around so I can signal to Alexei that we're leaving, but he's nowhere to be seen. I wonder if he's had second thoughts? Or just got distracted with something for work. I shrug and dart through the rain and puddles with Sarah to a smaller tent where she finds me some dry clothes, and a rigged changing room in the corner. I feel a million times better when I'm dressed again, and my hair dry. Of course, then I realize it's only going to get wet again when we leave, but Sarah surprises me with a funky yellow rain hat. Where it came from is anybody's guess because aside from the garish orange Hawaiian shirts meant to set off the officials, everything is black and camo.

We make another dash to yet a third tent which has more food set out and a bunch of folding chairs. When our plates are loaded, or as much as they can be when the offerings are bland sandwiches and still slightly green bananas, we sit down.

"So tell me all about meeting Alexei here because I swear the man you described to me in emails is nothing like what I saw in there."

"I know!" I gulp. "He's gotten all bossy and, um…" I'm not sure how to describe the rest of it.

Sarah gives me a knowing look and a secret smile. "I can guess. So apparently he's not oblivious to you after all?"

I shake my head, eyes wide. I'm still shocked by that revelation.

"So, did he just walk up to you and throw you over his shoulder? Or what?"

"Nooo… It started raining, so I sought shelter in this hut thing. Then I took my dress off because it was waterlogged and I thought I was alone. But I wasn't… and… well…"

Sarah throws her hand over her mouth to stifle a startled laugh. "No way! Then did he throw you over his shoulder?"

"Pretty much. He wanted to know why I left Florida."

"Are you going to go back with him? I'll miss you in Sala Bay but…"

I shake my head. "We didn't discuss it. Or a future

together. Not really. But Florida and I don't really get on that well. Weather-wise."

"Hmmm. Can I make a confession?"

I raise an eyebrow and wait her out.

"I knew he was going to be here. I had nothing to do with him being in the hut you wandered into but I might have known generally where he would be stationed." She's twisting her fingers together. "To be fair, the man you described was more likely to talk, not stalk, but..."

I gape at her. This was all a setup? But a well-intentioned one, I guess. If she thought I had feelings for him. Which I do, they're just really confused right now. "It's okay, Sarah. I'm just... It's been quite a day," I finish lamely.

"I'll bet. Maybe tomorrow when you see him, he'll be more like the sea of calm you remember." She sounds doubtful. And with good reason, because suddenly the energy in the tent shifts. We both glance up and there's Alexei, looking thoroughly wet and worried, scanning the tent. When his eyes find me, they blaze with ferocity. I can't tell if it's anger or passion or something else entirely. But whatever is, it's not calm and mild.

He stalks stiffly over to us, his eyes never leaving mine. Sarah might as well be invisible. When he's standing directly in front of me, his beautiful lips tighten as he takes the plate and soda can out of my hands, setting them on the ground. Then he deadlifts me out of the chair and, yes, flings me over his shoulder. All without a word. When he turns and starts walking back towards the entrance, I raise my head to see Sarah grinning and waving at me cheerfully. "Have fun!" she shouts after us.

There's a very firm and warm hand on my ass, holding me in place as Alexei carries me out of the tent and across a muddy field. It's not the most comfortable position, but it is giving me an opportunity to study the curve of *his* ass with the connoisseurship of a New York art critic. Five stars from me.

He stops abruptly and half slides me down his body, but not to the point where my feet touch the ground before bundling me into the passenger seat of a small beat-up pickup truck. He reaches over for the seatbelt before glaring at me briefly. "Stay put, Mia. I mean it." He secures the belt and shuts the door without another word. He's dripping wet and so am I. Again. But he walks around the front of the truck and gets in on the driver's side like it's a beautiful spring day and we're just going out for a drive. "Um, Alexei? Have you gone crazy? Why are you kidnapping me?"

He raises a sardonic eyebrow while sparing me a brief glance before returning his gaze front and center while starting the engine. "Believe I told you to let me know if you were leaving the tent," he says a little too calmly.

Now it's my turn to snarl a bit. "I looked for you, but you had disappeared. Makes that kind of hard doesn't it? And why should I, anyway? You don't own me."

"Wanna bet?"

I bite my tongue and look out the window. We're both too tense and wound up for this to go anyplace good right now.

There's an electric anticipatory silence as Alexei drives slowly down a rutted track. My cell phone pings from my small bag and I gratefully reach for it as a distraction. It's Sarah asking, **You okay? Totally loved your exit!** Followed by some emojis I don't understand and I suspect would make me blush if I asked. **Annoyed but fine**, I respond.

Good, your station's been changed for tomorrow. You're to report to the dock with Alexei.

You're kidding me? Right?

Nope. Decided over my head.

"Alexei, what did you do?" Warning laces my voice.

He doesn't turn his head. "I'm done waiting, Mia."

"What does that have to do with my job?"

"Nothing when it comes to moving fish. Everything

when it has to do with flirting with other guys."

Oh. He's jealous. It finally sinks in. That's kinda cute. In a possessive, controlling kind of way.

"What's it going to take for you to relax enough to know I'm not really looking at them?"

There's a long pregnant pause, before his usual good humor starts to show through the cracks. "I don't know. But several months solid fucking would be a good start."

At that, my panties go wet and I'm shifting awkwardly in the hard seat. Months spent in a bed with Alexei being all stern and possessive. Making sure I'm too overwhelmed with orgasms to want to leave. I lick my lips. "Um, okay?"

He grins briefly. "Glad to hear I don't have to fight you on that one at least."

I roll my eyes just as we pull into a narrow driveway lined with colorful plumeria trees. There's a beautiful small cottage with white plaster walls and a red tile roof sitting at the end. It's adorable even in the rain. And there's just a hint of deep blue beyond that suggests there might be a view of the sea. "You're staying here?"

"No. We are staying here. At least overnight. Belongs to a family member of an old colleague."

"What about food?" I didn't get very far on my plate of sandwiches before he dragged me out of there.

"I'm going to make sure everything is safe and then I'll leave you to get a bath while I go grab something from the store. It probably won't be exciting but we'll eat."

A bath sounds really heavenly right now. I sigh with longing and get out of the truck without waiting for Alexei. He frowns at me but follows me up to the small front porch. The door opens easily with his key, and I step gingerly inside. It feels like we're trespassing in someone's home, but a quick tour says it's clearly a vacation place. Stocked with the basics but there's not much personal lying around. A few photos and some seashells probably acquired at a nearby beach.

Alexei does a quick security check, even lifting the mattress in the master bedroom and poking at the back wall of the linen closet. What has this guy been doing for a living? Then he drops an absentminded kiss on my forehead before walking back out the door. I hear the truck engine fade away before I even move from that spot. It's a beautiful little house, but someone is going to have to make the bed up. And unless I missed something Alexei didn't bother bringing any luggage with, I don't know, clothes or other practical items. Does he expect both of us to just stay naked until we leave in the morning? My breasts grow heavy, heavier than normal, at the thought.

There's something about the air temperature and

humidity of Hawaii that makes going naked feel completely natural. I've never been nudist inclined. Before now, anyway. And it's not like I want anyone else to see me. But wandering around privately without clothes feels okay. So I shrug and go in to the spacious bathroom to start a bath.

The pipes creak a bit and it takes a few minutes for hot water to start flowing, but before long I'm eyeing the deep lounging tub full of steaming water with longing. I toss in a small handful of sparkling pink bath crystals I just can't resist and strip. The steamy air fills with the scent of gardenias. Stepping into the water is heaven. It would be sublime bliss if it came with a glass of wine and a romance novel. But then I realize I've got my own book in my head, namely Alexei who's face and body always take over the hero's no matter what I'm reading.

I lean back and just let myself go with the visions that come to me, sleeping in Alexei's arms, waking up to him, kissing me. I try to imagine what it would feel like to have his cock buried inside me, but I can't make it happen. I might be a virgin, but it's not like I don't own three different vibrators, so I'm not a stranger to the concepts. I just can't imagine him. There. Filling me completely. I want to though. So bad.

Alexei

I'll admit my brain isn't working at full capacity. Panic will do that to a man. Now that I've got Mia safe and dry and where we can talk without interruptions, I'm starting to relax a little bit. Enough to realize that we didn't bring any clothes or toiletries. So when I hit the tiny shopping center that serves as the gas station and grocery, I spend a bit more money than I'd planned. Because of course everything is five times what it would cost on the mainland. I'm sure locals have ways of making a dollar stretch but I don't have the luxury of figuring that out right now. They don't sell clothing, however, in any form and finally I decide, fuck it. We don't need clothes until tomorrow, anyway. And I'm hoping the food will make up for it.

After talking to the clerk for a few minutes I learn about a small farm stand where I can buy fresh fruit and fish if the catch has been good. So I head down that rural road, following directions as best I can. It's trickier reversing back to the cottage. But I've had plenty of experience navigating unmarked roads around the world, so only about an hour has passed when I pull back up in front of the small house. Hopefully, a little time by herself has restored Mia's equilibrium.

I'm not so sure when I unlatch the door and find her standing by the window that faces the ocean stark naked. Since I swallowed my tongue at the first glimpse of her shapely ass, it takes a second to get out a strangled, "Mia?"

She turns with a winsome smile. "Oh good, you're back. Did you find food?"

I nod woodenly. Her smile turns into a grin. "You forgot clothes."

Staring at her has my cock hard enough to burst. I need to feed her. *Food first* I lecture myself.

Mia's smile slips with concern. "Alexei? Are you okay?"

"I will be. Eventually."

Her gaze travels over my body before landing on the bulge tenting my pants. As if sensing her gaze, my cock surges forward.

"Oh," she laughs nervously. She half turns as if to go find her dress, but I stop her.

"Don't. I can't get enough of seeing you. All of you. You're beautiful, Mia, and if I had my way I'd keep you naked until you can see that for yourself."

She blushes and then pads over the tiled floors to place a soft kiss on my cheek. I turn and take her lips with mine. I want to drop the grocery bags but there's glass in there so I don't dare. This time, though, I don't have to chase after her, she's right there meeting my tongue with hers letting me know we're in this together.

"Oh, Alexei," she sighs.

"Let me put this stuff down," I mutter reluctantly.

She dances back, her grin returning. "What are you making?"

"Um… I mostly grabbed stuff that looked good. I didn't worry about combining it. Come see."

We head into the small kitchen off the living room. It opens onto a back terrace with a built-in barbeque and even though this is the back of beyond, it seems like people pop up out of nowhere in the islands. So I don't really want Mia wandering around out there sans clothing. Mind you, my brain has pretty much turned off because every bounce and jiggle has my cock throbbing painfully.

As soon as I set the bags down on the counter, my hands instinctively reach for Mia. She tenses slightly and then relaxes as I pull her close against me. Her skin is warm and silky smooth. I reach down to drop a kiss on her shoulder. "You're beyond beautiful, Mia."

Her gaze slants up to meet mine, a question shining through. I shrug absently. "No question or request there, sweetness. Just a statement of fact."

Her lips quirk minutely before she reaches for the buttons on my shirt, deftly going to work. I let her pull it off me, eager to remove any barriers between us. She moans softly as she presses her breasts into my chest. I reach a hand up to the middle of her back to hold her there. "What's your pleasure, Mia? Dinner? Bed? By which I mean making love. I sincerely hope you aren't thinking you're getting any sleep tonight."

Her eyes widen, the pupils expanding. "Um. Wow. You're kind of an all-or-nothing guy, aren't you?"

"There were reasons I couldn't claim you before, Mia. I can't explain all of them, but I'll do my best to brief you tomorrow. Believe me, if I had acted on my desires you'd be pregnant with our second child by now."

She swallows hard. "About that, I'm not on anything."

I nod stiffly. My entire body is hurting with the effort not to pound into her right here and now. "I have condoms but I'd rather take you bare, let you feel all of me against your virgin channel."

"And if I get pregnant?" Her voice is soft, mumbled against my chest where she's hiding her face once again.

I need her to see my sincerity, so I bring her chin up with a finger. "Mia. We're getting married as soon as I can figure out what state to file the paperwork in. As in less than thirty days at the outside. I could offer to pull out and reduce the risk, but I have zero desire to do that and I'm not entirely sure I'm capable of that much control around you. I want to fill you so full of cum it's dripping down your thighs for the next week. And since I fully intend to keep topping you up, I would think getting pregnant is more likely than not. Still your choice though."

She studies my face, her white teeth gnawing at her lower lip while she weighs pros and cons. Mia's probably doing some kind of logistical risk analysis before she rises up on her tiptoes and drops a small kiss on my lips. "Okay."

"Okay, meaning I can fuck you with nothing between us?"

She nods shyly. "Honestly, Alexei, I can't really believe we're having this conversation."

"We'd have had it sooner if you hadn't run away from Florida." I drop both hands to the perfect curve of her ass, pressing her center against my aching cock.

Her eyes glint with sass. "Or if you had bothered to come find me. Guess we're even on that score, huh?"

Instead of arguing, I kiss her deeply, thoroughly, until all I can see or smell or feel is Mia. She's panting slightly when I finally pull back to let us both breathe.

7

★ ★ ★

Mia

My head is spinning. Only this morning Alexei was this unobtainable dream in my mind, something I took out and cuddled with on the cold rainy nights in my cozy little apartment in Sala Bay. And now we're talking about having a baby? Or at least doing all the things that make one happen… And I swear I've spent most of the day naked and pressed up against him. Not that I'm complaining. He smells delicious, like orange and cinnamon with a healthy dose of warm man.

I'm beginning to understand that his clenched jaw and all have more to do with restraint around me more than control in general. I think I'm flattered? I'm not entirely sure. What I am sure about is that I have a deep-seated need to see the Alexei that isn't holding anything back. I'm a little nervous, I admit. But I want to see that. So bad! I don't think he's too far from his breaking point so it's a little bit like turning away from the pot of jam on the stove right before it starts spitting out burning hot splutters. Except with

Alexei, I think his losing control is going to feel good. Really good. And maybe that's why all of a sudden I'm completely comfortable being bare-ass naked in front of a man. Never saw that coming…

Somebody had better be the responsible person and put the perishable food away, though. Alexei's arms are caging me in against the counter, but I turn and start rifling through the bags anyway. Hmm, lots of fresh fruit, some fish. I hand the fish to him and point at the refrigerator. He looks like he's about to protest, but in the end he swivels and opens the fridge door, leaving it open while I hand him the small carton of milk and yogurt. There's a tiny bag of coffee and some foreign-looking vegetables that I hope he knows what to do with and that's about it.

"Sooo… bed?" I ask nervously.

His lips twitch ever so slightly. "Mia, despite appearances to the contrary, I'm not going to attack you. How about I feed you before I fuck your brains out?"

"With what we just put away?"

He shakes his head no. "Just fruit. In bed."

"Won't that be messy?"

"Yes." His eyes are bright with anticipation, and I decide I need to relax and let him do all the work. He clearly wants to and I've no objection.

"Okay, you're in charge, then. I'll be waiting." And

with that I sashay from the kitchen, my hips swinging with the knowledge that they're being watched and appreciated. Another first for me. I head into the bedroom where I pull back the top sheet I spread over the bed earlier. It's too warm for anything heavier, and settle myself against the white rattan headboard piled high with pillows. I try to arrange myself as attractively as possible but after five minutes I go back to my usual at-home-by-myself comfortable lounging position. I'm definitely not what anyone would call a femme fatale, but at the moment I feel like one.

I have a little too much time to anticipate what's coming. I don't know what took Alexei so long but it seems like forever before he appears in the bedroom doorway with a plate of cut up tropical fruit. There's no way I look like a vixen, the way the butterflies are dancing in my stomach. Without a word Alexei sets the plate down on top of the simple white dresser and strips with military efficiency. Admittedly, his chest was already deliciously bare, but this man is not self-conscious at all. And I can see why. He has zero reason to be embarrassed about *anything*. My mouth goes dry and my eyes are glued to his enormous cock. That won't fit.

I hear a patient sigh. "Mia?"

Eventually I drag my gaze up to meet his calm eyes. "What?"

"Trust me?"

"It's not you I'm concerned about."

His eyes smile even as his lips barely twitch.

"Okay, it's you, but not *you* you. That won't fit." I point at his cock, which is pointing back at me.

"It will. When you're ready."

I frown. And chew on my lip until Alexei's thumb gently pulls it down and away. "Alexei…"

"What?"

"You're bigger than my biggest toy. By a lot. And that one I never use because it hurts."

"Mia. What are you doing playing around with things that hurt?"

I shake my head. "Exactly. I don't. Not into that. I thought it might make up for, well the lack of the real thing in my life but I didn't like it."

"I promise you're going to like having me inside you, sweetness. So much you'll be begging me not to leave."

I don't want to call Alexei a liar exactly, and I do want him. I just don't think he understands that I'm obviously defective somehow in that department.

"Stop worrying. Here. Scoot over and have some mango."

He's trying to distract me and I let him, although my anxiety hasn't lessened. I think we're both going to be frustrated and embarrassed before the night is over, but clearly he's not going to take my word for it. So I sigh and slide over in the bed and he joins me, leaning against the headboard before reaching for the plate of fruit. I go to take a piece and he zips the plate out of my reach.

"My fruit, my rules," he says with mock sternness. He picks up a slim sliver of sunshiny yellow mango and holds it hovering over my lips, forcing me to reach for it and suck it in. If I want it, that is, and I do. A drop of juice escapes and runs down my chin. Alexei's mouth is there to stop it before I can blink. He licks and kisses my skin before dropping a small peck at the corner of my mouth. "Another?" he asks.

I nod, mesmerized.

He feeds me a chunk of pineapple, frowning when it doesn't drip at all. I grin at his scowl. "Too neat for you?"

"I have alternatives," he mutters and then squeezes a chunk over my breasts, watching in fascination as the juice splits and trails down into smaller rivulets. "Here," he says as he slides another slice of mango in my mouth before ducking his head and chasing each drop of juice, licking back up the trail it left behind. I shift on the bed, my clit is starting to throb and my own juices are making my thighs sticky.

Alexei feeds me a thick slice of golden kiwi then trails a line of passion fruit pulp across my belly. He takes his time consuming that one, tasting more of my skin than the fruit, I think. I had no idea I had so many nerve endings there, but by the time his dark head comes up, I'm quivering with need. My fingers thread through his dark hair with the urgent compulsion to hold on to something.

"Enough fruit for now?" his voice has descended an octave I swear.

"Yes, but…"

"Relax, Mia. All you need to do is feel." He slides down in the bed, kissing my hip.

That's the problem, really. I'm feeling too much. Well, that and the fact that his monster cock will split me in two. I must have said that out loud because there's a strangled laugh followed by, "It's not abnormally large, Mia, but thank you for the compliment."

I blush all over and I'm sure he sees that because his big hand dips between my legs, spreading them wide. "You're charming when you blush, baby. But you've nothing to be embarrassed about. I promised you'd be begging and you will be. Hold tight."

His head disappears between my thighs. I stare down at the back of it in bemusement. How did I get here again?

Alexei tugs me down farther on the bed so he can spread my thighs wider, and then he licks me from one end to the other. Everything in me pulses with building sensation.

Alexei

Mia's scent is tropical florals mixed with the citrusy aroma of the fruit I spread on her. I want to devour her, my hunger only amplified by the months, no, years of waiting. In theory, I should be holding off even now until I'm completely free of all my entanglements. Instead, I suck gently on her rosy little clit, watching her writhe with pleasure as she learns her body in ways she never has before. My angel is a fucking virgin. But not for much longer. She's all mine to worship and show her just how beautiful she is, inside and out. I wanted to laugh at her horror when she spied my cock for the first time. Her amazement and subsequent staring only serve to make it harder and thicker than ever. But she's so damn wet I could probably slide into her right now with a single thrust. I won't though. I want her relaxed and loose, with at least a few orgasms under her belt before we go there. Bringing her to that peak of pleasure is the best fucking mission of my life.

Besides, I'm having fun eating her out. Something I've dreamed of doing but wasn't positive she'd be comfortable with. She's always seemed somewhat shy and self-contained, but maybe that was partly due to her lack of experience. Regardless, Mia is perfection. It's like she's been made just for me, virgin pussy and all.

I part her delicate folds to tease her channel with the length of my tongue and Mia explodes, "Alex… ei!" Her entire body spasms as the first of many orgasms rips through her. Her muscles tighten and her fingers clutch at my head, spasming there rather than gripping anything. I'm not letting up now. I rake my teeth gently across her clit, already swollen with arousal and she twitches her hips, rotating side to side as she tries to both embrace and escape the flood of sensation. I nip her hip in warning to stay still. She makes an effort to tug me up, but I'm not done.

Sliding a finger into her slick channel, I watch her face. Her eyes are closed, she's breathing heavily, her lips parted. A second finger joins the first. "Mia, love? Tell me how that feels."

"So good. Want you, all of you." She's moaning as I slide my fingers in and out, teasing her with a slow, erratic rhythm. She brings her knees up, trying to trap my hand, eager to ride that pinnacle again.

"Soon, kitten. I want you to cum for me again. Can you do that?"

"Nooo. Too much," she whimpers, her beautiful hazel eyes open, pupils wide.

I pick up the pace, pausing to flick her clit every few strokes until I feel her pussy trying to grasp and hold my fingers. As I gently push a third finger in, I lean in to suck on her clit, bringing the sensitive nub back into my mouth and circling it with my tongue. Mia clenches down on my hand, her walls clasping my fingers with warm, wet heat. Her thighs against my head, soft and strong at the same time. Then she shatters, tightening and then releasing as pleasure racks her body with tiny tremors. I sooth her gently with light strokes, unwilling to simply pull out and leave her empty.

When she finally calms, I kiss my way back up her body, pausing only when I reach her lips. I wait for her eyes to open, bright with satisfaction.

Mia smiles. "Now what?"

"Now I truly make you mine. Are you ready for me?"

"Are you sure you're not going to break me?"

"I'm sure." I can't help smiling at her hopeful expression, although to her it might look more like a grimace because my cock is fucking throbbing with need, pre-cum leaking from the tip. Mia is soaking wet and about as relaxed as a human can get and still give consent. I line up with her entrance, nudging her pussy with just the tip of my cock. She sighs prettily and spreads her legs wide, accepting me into her body. I sink in, an inch at a time, the muscles in my back aching with restraint. But I don't want to rush this. For Mia's sake and my own, because she is fucking glorious. Sinking into her is like tasting a new favorite flavor of ice cream with every breath. Each time I think this is better than good ever gets, I sink a little further into her and *that's* better than before. She's gripping me like a glove and it has all my nerve endings tightening in anticipation.

"You're taking my cock beautifully, Mia. You feel like heaven. You're so damn tight, little one."

"So full, Alexei. Want all of you." She throws her head back as I sink in that final inch. Fully seated, I pause to let her catch her breath, to get used to the sensation of being truly stretched by a man's cock. And mine is the only one she's ever going to know. I mentally record a new resolve to eat better because damn if I'm going to die and leave her on her own. Before long, she begins to shift, her channel fluttering against my cock. I kiss her deeply, pleased with her willingness to take all of me despite her virginal misgivings and pull out even while her body tries to stop me.

Then, with a slow thrust of my hips, I'm once again rocking into her tight channel. My cock is slick with her cream, stretching her wide, as she trembles in response. I repeat this over and over, relishing the feeling of taking her bare until with a small scream Mia clenches around me. Harder than she did with my fingers, tightening her walls on my cock like a vise until I lose all control. With a roar, I pound into her, my cock spurting cum like a breach of the

Hoover dam. My vision goes white hot as I spill into her swollen pussy, coating her walls, filling her up with everything I've got. I feel her flying apart one more time beneath me, her graceful arms clutching at my back, nails biting into my shoulders as she gives way to her mounting release.

When I can see again, I slide out of her as gently as I can, flipping us over so I don't crush her and soothe her back down to earth. With a small sweet sigh, she nestles against my chest, and I let my eyes close.

8

★ ★ ★

Mia

I wake up groggy and sticky. In all my romance novels, this moment is characterized by long languorous kisses. Reality has my mouth feeling grotty. I need to pee, and my skin is apparently glued to Alexei. Pulling apart makes a loud squelching sound, which wakes him up. He blinks a few times and then grins sleepily at my blush. "Get used to it, Mia. Every morning from here on out."

"I'm going to be stuck to you like sitting on my grandpa's vinyl seats on a summer day?"

"Yes. We can always move to Alaska where it won't be so sticky but I really don't mind."

I turn away, flustered, and scurry into the adjacent bathroom. Once every part of me is fresh and clean, I feel a lot better. Stretching my arms up to wash my hair makes me notice the pull of my abdominals, and that brings the memories of Alexei pulsing inside me back in full force. My pussy clenches and my legs go weak at the knees. So when he steps into the shower behind me, it feels perfectly natural to turn and reach my arms around his neck.

He kisses me, his hands palming my ass and holding me against his semi-erect cock. I quiver with excitement. Now that I know what all the fuss is about, I could easily become addicted. "Can we do this every morning too?"

"Absolutely." He brings his hands back up to thread his fingers in my hair. Tilting my head back, he uses them to rinse the shampoo out before swinging me around to press me against the white tile.

"How sore are you?" he asks gently.

I shrug. "Not really? Like a good gym workout but I'm not in pain if that's what you're asking."

"Thank fuck." He lifts my left leg by the thigh, bringing it up around his waist. The slope of the old-fashioned tub means I'm leaning back slightly, so I hold on tight to his shoulders. Before I can catch my breath, his cock is sliding into my welcoming pussy. I sigh with satisfaction, loving the warm sensation of Alexei inside of me, against me, all around me.

"Still worried it won't fit?" he inquires, laughing.

"No!" I hide my blushing face against his chest. My position means I can't really move without losing my balance, so Alexei has to do all the maneuvering. He's in no hurry. The movement of his cock is like the tide coming in at the beach, gradually increasing in tempo and force without startling. His right hand grips my hip as he fucks me slowly and deeply. Waves of pleasure wash over me, gradually building to a crescendo that has me closing my eyes. I want to hold on to that feeling but before I'm ready Alexei pushes deep and I'm flying apart. My climax is like an undertow, dragging me beneath the waves and rolling me around until I have no strength left. At the same time Alexei cums, pulsing fiercely deep inside me as I sink bonelessly down onto him. I can feel him filling me with his seed, every nuance and crevice imprinted with him in one form or another.

His heart beats steadily under my cheek while I try to adjust to this new plane of existence. He settles me against him, lowering my leg gently and kissing my neck with small sweet touches.

"Never going to let you go, Mia. You're mine forever, kitten." His murmur is fierce in my ear, and I press closer against him, needing those words.

I don't know how much time has passed but I can feel the water turning cold against Alexei's back so I reluctantly pull back. "We should get out. I think we used up all the hot water."

He nods, looking reluctant, but he bends down and gently rinses his cum from my pussy and thighs before turning off the water and helping me out of the tub. When I reach for a towel, he stops me and proceeds to rub the water from my skin in a way that has me all tingly again by the time he's done. "Don't we have jobs to get to?" I inquire wryly.

He smiles at me with sleepy satisfaction. "We're together all day, Mia. Don't be thinking I'm going to keep my hands to myself while we're out there alone together."

Somehow I've created a monster. But I'm not all that unhappy about it.

Then a sudden unpleasant thought hits me. "Um, I don't have anything to wear but the stuff from yesterday."

"How about you wear my shirt again and we'll stop by your tent and collect your things before we go to our station. You're staying with me from here on out, anyway."

"Oh, I am, am I?" I wonder how long before his high handedness goes from adorable to annoying?

"Yes. You don't strike me as the sort that likes public sex, and that's your other option." He drops a matter of fact kiss on my lips before turning into the kitchen and starting the coffee maker.

I gape after him. No. I'm definitely not the girl that wants to be watched like that, but since when did those become my only two options? I don't exactly want Alexei out of my sight either, so maybe I should be careful what I ask for.

Instead of his shirt, I shake out my clothes from yesterday. The world is going to have to get by without me wearing underwear, though, until I can get back to my luggage. Alexei's eyes go a little glassy when he turns and sees the curve of my unsupported breasts. "Fuck, Mia. You make me want to strip you and start all over again."

Me too. I twine my arms around him and press my tits against his chest. Their softness unencumbered and free. Alexei leans down for a deep kiss. I'm breathless by the time our lips part just as the coffee maker beeps with success.

Mia

Alexei and I manage to eat breakfast without falling back into bed, but I admit I thought about it. Except I'm truly starving. A few pieces of fruit last night were not enough to keep me going today, although I don't regret for a minute skipping a real dinner in favor of being full of Alexei. So now we're nibbling on the various bits and pieces he found at the tiny grocery store last night. I wouldn't exactly describe it as a particular dish. It's not like sitting down to an omelet. More like a little fruit, some yogurt, a handful of nuts.

And I don't care in the least because I'm already looking forward to tonight. And the best part is my calm, patient Alexei is back. His olive green eyes promising restful shelter, like a mossy corner in the deep woods. I can't hold it in. I wrap my arms around his middle and bury my face in his rock-hard chest.

He doesn't seem to mind but his questioning,

"Mia?" has me looking up to see his gorgeous smile, the same one that sent me scurrying off to Washington when I saw it aimed at another woman. Only this time I'm the one basking in his attention.

"Just happy," I say lightly. I'm in love with him but that seems too big a statement to make over breakfast. Or maybe he already knows it? I sigh and snuggle against him again. He smells divine and I'm confused as to how he made that happen because he doesn't have any of his things with him, either. Maybe it's simply him. In which case I'm doomed because I won't be able to resist sniffing him constantly.

Reluctantly we leave the cottage a few minutes later, locking up behind us and make the thirty-minute drive back to the games compound. Alexei drives straight through, except for the checkpoints, circling around the back until we find the Vixen tent. "Why the heck do they have you way out here?" He sounds bewildered.

"Beats me. Better stay here, they might not all be dressed yet."

Alexei looks ready to argue but then must see the potential for disaster and nods before sitting back, leaving the engine running. I guess that's my hint not to linger while chatting. At least today the sky is clear and blue, so I don't have to dash between raindrops.

When I enter the tent, even though I know it's only five women, I swear the way they're dashing to and fro between curling irons and mirrors that it seems like twenty. As soon as the first one spots me she grins and starts slow clapping and then the others join in.

"Heard you bagged a live one, Tennant. Nice going on your first day!"

Oh my God. I blush and duck my head. "Oh, um." I mean, what do you say to that? I dart for my cot with my suitcase underneath it, hoping to grab it and escape, but of course these girls now consider themselves pros and block me.

"Spill, girl. Who is he?"

"*How* is he?" interjects another saucily.

I roll my eyes. "*He* is waiting outside and I've known him for years, so no spying skills involved. I'm sorry but I've got to hurry. And surely you're all late too?" I raise an inquiring eyebrow, hoping to move them on. It doesn't work, but they do let me walk out with my wheelie suitcase rumbling behind me. Mostly because they've all run to the flimsy door to get a good look at Alexei. Friendly cat calls and laughter follow me out as I blush harder. Alexei gets out to take my suitcase from me, his eyes asking if I need help with the rowdy crowd, but I shake my head infinitesimally and we get back in our ratty borrowed vehicle.

We don't talk as Alexei guides the old truck down the rutted dirt road towards our destination. But every now and then he brings my left hand up to his mouth for a quick kiss, almost as if he can't believe I'm sitting next to him. All without taking his eyes off the road. Which means I get to study his elegant profile to my heart's content. I still can't quite believe he's all mine. It feels like a shoe is about to drop and I'll wake up to discover it was all a dream.

Maybe it's because I'm slightly on edge that I notice a vehicle keeping a careful distance behind us. The road is so curvy that it only comes into glimpse once or twice but it never comes closer, which seems odd. It's making me nervous.

"Alexei?"

"Hmmm?" He briefly turns his green eyes my way.

"I think we're being followed."

He glances up at the rear-view mirror before looking skeptically back at me. "What makes you think that?"

At least he didn't come right out and say I'm imagining things. "Now and then I see a black SUV when the road straightens out, it's always the same distance behind us."

He frowns slightly. "I'll keep an eye out."

But then we're pulling up to the area beside a small dilapidated dock with an equally dingy boat tied to it. "We have to sit on that thing?" I ask in dismay. It looks like it smells. Badly. Probably of fish left out in the sun.

"Let's go take a look. Maybe it won't be that bad." Even Alexei sounds like this might be a step too far.

We get out of the truck and walk down the rickety dock. Alexei won't let go of my arm. I think he's afraid I'll fall over the edge or through a gap or something. When we get closer to the boat, I'm shocked it's still floating. There's a big hole just above the waterline.

"Hell if you're getting on that deathtrap, Mia. Let's head back. Something's wrong with this whole scenario." Worry tinges his voice, although I can tell he's trying not to let it show.

★ ★ ★

Alexei

The back of my neck is tingling with warning. That isn't the boat Lukas described to me. Not even close. And he's not the sort to embellish this kind of stuff. How many vodkas he can shoot? Yeah, he's a lightweight drinker, but not the way he talks about it.

This though? This has fuck up written all over it. And I have a clue who's behind it when I glance over my shoulder to see two goons getting out of a black SUV. Mia called it. But that's not going to keep her safe, and right now that's my number one concern.

I glance into the water. It's high tide so it should be deep enough for her. "Mia," I say as quietly and calmly as I can, "I want you to jump off the dock and swim under it. Wait until everyone is gone before coming out. Got it?"

"Why would I want to do that?" She's bewildered until she turns. "Oh. Who are they?"

"Bad guys." I don't move my lips, the stare down

with the foreign agents having already begun.

"Then you need my help," Mia insists.

"Jump, Mia. Now."

Instead she edges closer to my side. I don't like this and I'm torn about what to do about it. If Mia were an innocent bystander, I'd push her off the dock and apologize later. If I were still alive to do so. That anyone tracked me here means they probably already know about her and what she means to me. And it's not like I have any weapons on me. I haven't carried one in years. I'm attached to a cyber warfare unit and all the nasty stuff takes place with keystrokes not bullets. E-battles can be just as deadly in a different way, but it's not something I can whip up and deploy here.

"Fuck. Mia, please." I push her behind me as best I can.

She doesn't say anything, just gasps when the two men who are both sporting white blond crew cuts with dead looking eyes walk up to us.

The goon on the right slaps me on the shoulder. "Alexei, my old friend. So glad you could make it." The sting wouldn't have even been noticeable if I hadn't been anticipating it. Fuck. I feel all my worries fading away as the sunlight sparkles on the water. So pretty. Fuck!

Faintly, I hear Mia's voice going strident. Can't she

see what a beautiful day it is? She should be singing and laughing on the beach. I turn to tell her that, but I can't seem to move my head.

"No, he's not going anywhere without me. What did you do to him?" Her words wash over me. My Mia, so beautiful.

The two Russian agents lead me back to the SUV. I'm not unconscious, but I might as well be because I don't seem to care about anything besides watching the waves. A tiny part of my brain is panicking, but I can't figure out why. Mia trails behind. Didn't I tell her to go for a swim? She should do that. "Go for a swim," I tell her again, but my words are garbled, and she starts crying. That's not right.

Mia

My heart is in my throat, but I have to stay strong for Alexei. I have to save him and me both because I won't be able to figure out how to rescue him without going with these two cartoon villains as well. They don't seem to want me along, but they're not actively preventing me from getting in the back seat of the SUV with Alexei, either. I don't exactly see that as a good sign. He's clearly the one they were after and they appear to want him alive and conscious or they could have just shot us both at the dock. Why don't we have real guns again? And how did they find us way out here, anyway?

I snuggle against Alexei's side in the back seat, pretending to be his caring girlfriend who thinks he's suddenly taken sick. And who also isn't very smart since apparently I've completely forgotten that he was just fine before the two of them showed up. I might as well take advantage of how most men perceive me and make it work for us.

My eyes and ears are working overtime trying to figure out what's going on and how to get both of us out of it in one piece. What the hell did they give him? Asking probably won't help. And I doubt they'd tell me how long it's going to be before whatever it is starts wearing off. They seem like the type to already have a second dose ready and I don't want to tempt them to use it on me.

Alexei starts singing some weird song I've never heard before — at least not how he's singing it. I can't even tell what language it's in, he's slurring his words so badly.

"You. Girlfriend. Shut him up." One of the goons shouts back at me without turning his head. Fuck. I turn Alexei's face to me. His pupils are huge and I swear somewhere in there is a little spark of fear. He's worried about me. Even drugged up to the gills, there's a part of him that just can't stop being all bossy protective. He's in no state to reason with, so I do the one thing I can think of to stop him belting out show tunes. I kiss him.

There are four people in the vehicle and I'm the

only woman. That difference is obvious. But three of the four people think I don't understand Russian and they're wrong. I've never told anyone I started learning it. Not a soul. Because I'm really bad at it. The speaking part anyway, and I'm completely illiterate when it comes to the Cyrillic alphabet. But it was all part of my fantasy involving Alexei, who I always knew was bilingual even if he's never, ever said a word of Russian in my presence. Or even said something with an accent. But I didn't want to be that girl in the romance novel when the guy whispers sweet nothings in her ear that she doesn't understand. I wanted to not miss a moment. So I got one of those free language apps and practiced. For the amount of time I've put in, I ought to be qualified as an interpreter by now, but there's no chance of that.

But at least I can understand when Goon One turns to Goon Two and says, "maybe we should wait until tomorrow to get rid of her. It's going to be awhile before we get to fuck a woman again." I'm guessing on the 'fuck' because those language apps never teach you the juicy words but the way Goon One licked his lips I'm pretty confident on my translation. In some ways this is bad news but the upside is I know I have at least twelve hours or so to get the two of us out of this mess. And maybe Alexei will be able to help towards the end of that. I keep my head turned away, still kissing him softly, but with my ears tuned to the front seat.

They've sunk into raunchy vocabulary I don't understand, but I do catch the words for food and pissing. Okay. They must be considering a rest stop, probably at a convenience store because I don't think the Hawaiian highway department is that concerned about sleepy cross-country drivers out here.

If I can get them to leave us alone in the car, I might be able to get us out of this soon. Because I have other talents I never get to use. Namely, I can hot wire a car in less than five seconds. But I've never actually done it outside of a classroom setting.

I settle against Alexei's chest, soothing him with small hand motions while pretending to be asleep. I'm not sure how convincing I am because my nerves are strung tight. It seems to work though. When the car finally rolls to a stop, I don't look up to see where we are. I just wait. The two men argue for a minute quietly. Something about 'catching attention' and then 'stupid girl'. I hold my breath. Eventually they get out and shut the doors. The electronic beep of the lock being activated sounds unbearably loud. I force myself to wait thirty seconds to make sure they're well away from the vehicle before pulling away from Alexei and hurling myself into the front seat. My head is down below the steering wheel, reaching for wires before my butt hits the seat. And I haven't lost my touch.

The engine roars to life and I bring my head up as my hands reach for the steering wheel. They didn't even bother to set the parking brake. I slam on the gas, fishtailing out of the small gravel parking lot. The seatbelt is going to have to wait even though I feel incredibly guilty driving without it. I have no idea where we are, but there's no mistaking the two men who run from the equally small gas station waving their arms. If one of them has a gun, I don't pause to find out. I keep driving in the direction they were headed until I see a road that looks big enough not to dead end in a hurry and turn right.

Alexei starts singing again, something cheerful. My adrenalin is up and the sun is shining so I shouldn't be too surprised when a small smile curves my lips, but I am.

I'm not this woman, the one that loves adventure, escaping bad guys like a low-budget movie. My brain gets busy figuring out how to keep us from falling back in with the goons because I'm pretty sure if that happens they won't be treating me like the idiot girlfriend any longer.

We need to ditch the car, but somewhere where we can make a getaway to another destination to put some distance between us and it. I'm sure they have trackers all over it and I doubt those two are the only bad guys on the island. Then the road ahead widens abruptly and suddenly we're in a town. There. A grocery store. Not quite as huge as one on the mainland, but close. If I park the car there, they might spend five minutes looking for us in the store. I park and am just about to undo the wires keeping the engine running when I have a burst of inspiration. If someone were to steal the car, then it would drive to yet another destination. I like it. I unlock the doors and even roll down the driver's side window to encourage a would be thief before getting out and going around to fetch Alexei.

The bad guys took both our cellphones and my small purse but I think… yes… they left his wallet in his pants pocket. I fish it out, rolling my eyes slightly when the man of my dreams leans in for a sloppy kiss. I give him a quick peck because I can and because he's adorable when high out of his mind, even if I am worried about him. And I certainly hope he's never in this condition again. Then I lead him away, scanning the surroundings for our next destination. That's when I spy a small transit bus coming up the road. This town doesn't look big enough to need public transit so it must be an all-island type of thing. Perfect.

I position Alexei by the bus stop I spy at the corner of the grocery store parking lot and rifle through his wallet for a few bills. It can't be too expensive, can it? The bus grinds to a halt with a loud squeal and a giant electronic sigh as the doors swing open. I have to half drag Alexei up the few stairs and then help him collapse on the bench seat at the front.

"How much?" I ask the driver.

"Where you headed?" he asks in return.

"Our car broke down. Is there a town with a hotel where we can get a room?"

He nods. "Five bucks. I'll let you know when it's your stop."

I fold a five-dollar bill sufficiently to get it in the small, old-fashioned money collector and sit down next to Alexei. The bus pulls away with a jerk just as I spot a teenager opening the door to the SUV. Oh dear, I don't want a kid to get into trouble with those guys. Now I'm worried. But then a bigger nasty man with tattoos pushes him away and gets in. Okay. That guy can handle himself. I breathe a sigh of relief as the bus leaves town from the other end than the one we came from, and we're back in the open jungle of the countryside.

10

★ ★ ★

Mia

I'm a nervous wreck. The handful of passengers on the bus all look bored, like they're completely used to this lumbering bus and so over it anything will do for excitement. So I try not to keep frantically looking out the window. We already stand out. Everyone else looks like they're locals. And this isn't exactly the main route for tourists. I'm worried that Alexei is coming down from the high of whatever the goons gave him. Not that I don't want him getting that shit out of his system, but I've no idea what to expect. I certainly can't carry him.

So it's a big sigh of relief when the driver pulls to a rattling stop in another small town by a half-twisted pole that I'm guessing was once a bus stop sign and nods at me in the mirror. "Lady? This is your stop. Hotel is one block to the right. Tell them Hiko sent you."

He doesn't smile, but his eyes are friendly so I breathe a heart-felt "Thank you!" as I tug and haul

Alexei into an upright position. It's difficult and his eyelids are hanging heavy. I'm not sure if we should stay in this hotel or not, but what other options do I really have? I can't carry him and we can't sleep on the beach. So the hotel seems like the safest of the options. Maybe in a few hours he'll be more alert and we can relocate to where the bad guys can't find us.

Thankfully, it's a short block to the small hotel that looks like something from a mid-century postcard. The time when tiki bars were fashionable and Hawaiian hotels went out of their way to look like exotic huts instead of high-end condos. It's quaint and a little run down. I'm willing to bet it's family run and a little part of me is excited to see a bit of real Hawaii. Besides the bus. That was pretty real, too.

The lobby is empty, and after I ring the small bell on the desk, I get a few minutes to look around. It's clean and tidy and I think someone had fun rummaging in the attic because it's full to the gills of those oddities you would need for a 1950s tiki bar. Most of them are clearly not Hawaiian but 'islandesque' in style.

A young woman with long dark hair who barely looks out of her teens comes in from the back and looks surprised to see us. Maybe it's the way Alexei is leaning on my shoulder. "Hi," I start before she can ask any awkward questions. "My boyfriend isn't feeling well. Is there any chance we can get a room so he can get some rest?"

"Um, sure. We have plenty of vacancies. He doesn't need medical attention, does he? Because there isn't a doctor for about thirty miles."

"I don't think so. He should be fine." My fingers are crossed because what if he does need a doctor? But I have no idea what they gave him and his pulse rate seems fine so… I fill out the paper form she hands me with vague information and hand her cash from Alexei's wallet. Thankfully, she doesn't ask to see ID, which I think technically she's supposed to do. I gave our names as Miranda Williams and Albert Walker. Poor Alexei doesn't look anything like an Albert but I needed something similar in case I had to call him by name. "Oh, and is there anyplace to get food nearby?" I ask the clerk as I try to turn him towards the side door she directed me to.

"The tiki lounge opens at six. Other than that there's a small grocery down at the corner." She nods and turns to go back behind the beaded curtain.

Oh dear, that doesn't leave a lot of food options. I'd better get Alexei settled first. I half-haul him down the short corridor and past the few doors at the back of the building to our room, 107. The key slides in easily, and I smile when I see the room.

It's beautiful, smooth white tile on the floor and bamboo furniture with thick cushions in azure blue. Nothing tiki or retro about this space at all. The bed is dressed with white linens and a light white spread with gauzy netting hanging down from a fixture on the ceiling. I love it. With a grunt Alexei collapses on the bed and I suddenly realize he was working hard to try to help me get him to this point. I wonder how conscious he is?

Not now, of course, because I think he's out. His knees are bent so his feet are on the floor, which can't be comfortable in the long term, but he's too heavy for me to lift. So I take each foot and unlace his shoe before standing there studying him. He's breathing evenly and quietly. I mentally debate and then grab his wallet from where I set it on top of the TV. I'd better get us food and something with electrolytes for him to drink when he wakes. I'm guessing he's going to need it. I don't dare give him anything stronger because I don't know how it would react with what's in his system. Quietly as possible, I shut the door behind me and test the lock. He should be safe for a few minutes, but I'm going to do the shopping as fast as I can manage.

Luckily (I guess?) the store is tiny, and it only takes ten paces to cover the length of each wall so I can quickly see what they have and make my selection. The dinner options aren't great but I noticed there was a small coffeemaker in the room so I grab some instant noodle cups. It might taste a little strange but it should be edible even if it has a bit of coffee flavor. Some potato chips and some fruit, along with the sports drink for Alexei, and I'm good. All told, I've shopped, paid, and made it back to the room in under ten minutes.

As near as I can tell, he didn't move a muscle while I was gone. I double check that the deadbolt is fastened on the door. And then for good measure I move one of the bamboo chairs under the door handle. Not that it would keep even a small child from pushing open the door, but I figure the sound scraping across the tile might wake me up in the middle of the night. I check the windows too — making sure the locks are tight and the curtains are fully drawn. Mostly I'm fiddling, wasting time while keeping one eye on Alexei. He's not moving at all. So of course I have to put one knee on the bed so I can bend over and check his pulse. Just as I'm doing that, strong arms clamp on to me and bring me down beneath him. His eyes are still closed. I struggle as gently as I can manage, trying to free myself without hurting him, but he's having none of it.

"Alexei," I whisper softly, "let me go, love."

He doesn't answer, just sort of rolls into me and crushes his face into my neck. His arms are tight bands around my hips and back. At least now his feet are up on the bed, so he must be more comfortable. I stroke his back where I can reach, and he settled further into me with a long sigh.

Ten minutes later and I'm able to squeeze out from under him. My arm's gone numb, but I'm relieved to see him looking more normal, even if he is still asleep.

Alexei

My swim back to consciousness is difficult and exhausting. When I finally open my eyes, the world is dark. It takes a few frantic blinks for me to realize it's night, and my heart starts furiously beating in panic. Mia. Where is she? Did they hurt her? I move to swing my legs over the bed so I can go find her. Save her. But they hit something soft on the way. A soft moan echoes in the stillness. My fingers hunt for a light switch, feeling up the nightstand and the wall before finding a tiny toggle. The dim light of the delicate table lamp illuminates Mia's tousled curls. She's here. She's safe.

I keep repeating those words while trying to gulp air into my seizing lungs. She's here. She's safe. I touch her arm just to make sure. She's warm. She's here. She's safe. I close my eyes in relief and sink back down on the bed. In the dark again I can't be sure, so I pull her over against me as gently as I can. I don't know what she did while I was out, but I'm sure it was nothing trivial and she must be exhausted. Feeling her heart beat against my arm soothes me, and I fall back into sleep. Mia. My Mia.

I wake again when Mia tries to slip out of my arms. "Mia?" I ask without opening my eyes as I let her lift my arm off her hip.

"Relax, Alexei. Everything's fine for the moment. But it won't be if you don't let me go to the bathroom." Her voice is half-laugh, half-exasperation. It's music to my ears. I release her, but my eyes pop open to track her movements. I don't recognize this room. I want to ask her questions, but she's already gone.

Sighing, I sit up, and my head starts to pound like a motherfucker when I do. I'm sitting there trying to hold my skull together with my fingers when Mia comes back.

"Alexei, you alright?"

"Maybe, not sure. What happened yesterday?"

"How much of it do you remember?"

"It's fuzzy. You and I were on a dock…"

"Yeah." Her voice has gone soft with concern as she gently swipes her palm over my forehead. "Some bad Russian dudes showed up and injected you with something nasty."

"What?" I ask sharply.

"I have no idea, but it made you silly giddy for a while and then really toasted, sleepy sort of. You collapsed when I got you here, dead to the world. But at least you waited until there was a bed."

Fuck. Must have been something experimental. Those symptoms don't sound like any of their known agents, unless I just happen to have a weird reaction to something. "Did anyone hurt you? Did *I* hurt you?" The thought sends horror through my veins.

"No, love. You didn't. But they're still out there somewhere and I think they'd really like to hurt both of us."

I nod, keeping the movement as minimal as possible because fuck my head. "How did we get here?"

"I stole the car while they went in to use the bathroom. Then I drove until I could ditch it in a parking lot and get us on a bus. The bus dropped us off here."

She makes it sound simple, but I'm impressed. I drag one eye open to smile at her with pride. "Proud of you, kitten."

"Aw shucks." Mia grins, but her blush is adorable. "Do we need to stay here another night? I only booked it for one."

I shake my head no. "Too dangerous. Money?"

"Your wallet took care of us. They took both our phones."

Okay, I need to get my brain in gear. Anything else, and I'm putting us both in danger. I straighten, slowly. This time things go better. "Any coffee?"

"Hotel variety. Here." She hands me a mug, and I sip cautiously. It's not the worst. I wait to see if I have any reaction, but mostly the cobwebs seem to be clearing slightly. I sip some more and Mia gives me a cup of instant noodles already perking in hot water. "Sorry, it's the best I could do for food."

I nod gratefully. I've definitely started the day with worse. "I'm sorry I dragged you into this, that wasn't supposed to happen."

"You were expecting them?"

I shake my head, my mouth still full of noodles, but I'm too quick with the motion and a piercing ache starts behind my right temple. "Fuck. No, not exactly. I can't tell you everything but they're why I was waiting to come find you. I didn't want to drag any trouble behind me that could affect you. Another few weeks and the time limit will be up and I'm of no use."

"Time limit?" She sounds skeptical, like she thinks I'm still hallucinating.

"I never really left the military, Mia. I was partially detached for... plausible deniability I guess you might say. Government contractors can get away with certain things that military personnel can't. But the reality is what I was working with has a short shelf life. All sides pretty much acknowledge that six months out of the game and you no longer know anything useful."

I can feel her thinking that through as she sits down beside me. "You'd better not be about to tell me that you're leaving me behind for my own good."

My grin is automatic. "Wouldn't dare. Besides, I think we're 1, 0. You're better at saving me than vice versa. Maybe I'm too old." I shrug.

"For me or all the spy stuff?"

"Both, but I'm too selfish to let you go at this point. You're stuck with my sorry old ass."

She snorts in disbelief. "Your ass is perfectly fine, and you know it. So now what?"

"You were the one studying up on being a spy. What would you do?"

"Steal a yacht and head for the Caribbean?"

"Wrong ocean, and I don't think we need to be quite that dramatic. How about we call for help?"

"It can't be that easy. Besides, what if they're in on it?"

I sigh. She's got the bug of excitement clearly and isn't willing to let it go anytime soon. "Because Lukas and I go way back and he has no desire to give up his weekly golf game in Arizona for Moscow."

"Isn't he the one that sent us there in the first place?" Nope, she's not letting this go.

"Sort of. Will it make you happy if we call someone else?"

"Maybe Will? But I don't have his number or I'd

have called last night."

"He the guy with your friend?"

"Yeah, he plans these games every year. That's his job."

"Fine. We'll call him." And I'll be making some more top secret calls for extraction too.

Mia

I should be glad Alexei is treating me like an equal in all this and a tiny part of me is. But it's dwarfed by the part that worries he's not okay after what those guys did to him. I mean, where's my possessive alpha, take-charge, throw-me-over-his-shoulder guy? And is he coming back? I want *that* guy to say, "Mia, you're a fabulous spy."

This Alexei is sweet and certainly not stupid, but he's clearly hurting and I'm worried about him. So the sooner I can get him some trustworthy medical attention, the better. And then maybe I'll be the one to tie him to a bed somewhere so I can keep him safe and out of trouble. I snort laugh at the thought of bossing Alexei around like that. He raises one aristocratic eyebrow in a way so familiar I choke up. It's going to be okay. We're going to be okay.

"Something funny?"

"Yes, thinking about how to keep you safe and out of trouble in the future. I guess barefoot and pregnant is out?"

"Not for you." He says it so matter-of-factly, I almost miss the tiny twitch at the corner of his mouth. I roll my eyes in response.

"So, how are we calling for help? Neither of us have phones and there's nothing in the room."

"Front desk, I guess." He shrugs like it's no big deal. I don't even know what town we're in. How am I supposed to explain that to whoever picks up the phone at ACI without sounding like an idiot who's drunk too much fermented pineapple juice?

"Come here, Mia." His order is stern but level.

I walk over to him cautiously from where I was pacing by the window. He pulls me down on his lap. He's still weak. I can feel it in his arms, but you wouldn't know it from the way he's looking at me. "Stop worrying."

I smile a bit sadly. Until yesterday it never occurred to me to worry about him, not really. Because he always seemed so confident and always knew just what to do.

Kissing him softly, I whisper in his ear, "I love you. I'm going to worry. Get used to it."

When I turn back, his eyes are blazing. His hands clench on my hips. "You'd better get a lot of sleep tonight, Mia, because once I've over this crap I'm fucking you until I'm dry."

"Promise?"

He grins. "Promise. And I love you too. You know that, right?"

"Doesn't hurt to hear it ever few years."

"Come on — let's go make that phone call."

There's nothing to pack since we didn't arrive with any luggage. And we ate all the food I bought last night, or at least as much of it as we were ever going to. Alexei and I walk back towards the lobby, retracing the route from yesterday. Everything looks different now with Alexei being fully mobile and where I'm not so worried about him passing out at my feet. I'm still spinning my head right and left, checking for any lurking bad guys, though.

The lobby is cool and calm. It's empty of people. When I spy the clock on the wall half hidden by all the tiki warriors, I'm less surprised. It's already after ten.

An older woman steps out from behind the beaded curtain this time, already armed with a gracious smile. Alexei asks to borrow the phone and I watch as he enters a flurry of digits, reads off our location from the brochure on the counter and then hangs up. Maybe I don't really have a handle on this whole spy thing because he didn't say anything else. Just the address. Who was he talking to?

He smiles slightly when he glances over at me,

but doesn't respond to any of the questioning vibes I'm radiating. He hands the woman our room key, saying, "Thank you. We appreciate your hospitality last night." Then he takes my hand and leads me out through the main doors to wait in front of the building.

"Shouldn't we wait inside? You know, out of public view?"

That eyebrow goes north again as he turns to look down at me. "Mia? What exactly is public about a private rural driveway completely obscured by vegetation?"

I shrug. "I don't know. What about drones?"

"That would imply they already know where we are."

Yeah, I guess that's true. "So, who is coming for us? You didn't say anything."

"And I can't now either. Someone will be here shortly."

And he's right. I'm not sure what I was expecting. More black SUVs or maybe a white panel van if they're trying to hide in plain sight. I probably do watch too much TV because what arrives is a cranberry red sedan that's at least twenty years old and looks like something only a grandma would willingly drive. I'm more shocked by that than I was by the nasty Russians (who would have fit right in my favorite TV show without having to even change clothes).

It's not a grandma that emerges from the car though. It's a really good-looking man, almost as handsome as Alexei, and I guess my sucked in breath didn't go over so well in certain circles because Alexei's muscle tone is much improved. Based on the arm tightening around my waist, anyway.

The man's face is expressionless, but that just makes his chiseled jaw that much more architectural. He's tall, an inch or so shorter than Alexei, but that's nothing to complain about and his dark blond hair is just tousled enough to look natural. I wonder if it is?

"Price?" He asks in a deep baritone, again without inflection.

Alexei responds, "Affirmative."

And that's the extent of the conversation. Alexei opens the rear passenger door for me and shuts it once I'm seated. To my surprise, he gets in up front with the strange man instead of coming around to join me. The man hands him a narrow envelope.

Alexei flips through the contents as the car pulls out onto the small country road, sighs heavily and then tucks the envelope into the glove compartment. I'm dying with curiosity back here, but he doesn't even turn around. I'm not sure what speaking up might do to the current dynamic so I stay silent as

I assess. It worked with the bad guys but this is... different.

Alexei

This is going to be tricky. My only real option was to call a special hotline for extraction but that's going to come at a price. Namely, extensive debriefing where Mia is likely to be considered dangerous collateral. That she's even here with me now is almost certain to result in quite a bit of yelling.

I'm feeling much more myself but still not 100%. The first thing they're going to try to do is separate us, and I'm not sure how much leverage I have to keep that from happening. Our escort, who I vaguely recognize as one of the Ellis brothers, but which one I couldn't tell you, is sticking to the standard script. Which is, as anyone might guess, blank. Fuck.

If this were Vegas, I'd make him swing by a wedding chapel so we could get married now. That would at least afford Mia some legal rights. Maybe not enough, but they'd be more careful.

As it is, I'm going to have to use what little leverage I have. Briefly I look back at her from the reflection in the side mirror. She looks anxious and worried. She's had a helluva few days. A better man would walk away from her. Let her move on to a more normal life without the drama.

I'm not that man. I'm selfish as fuck when it comes

to Mia. And I'm willing to walk on broken glass to keep her safe, as long as it doesn't involve letting her go.

We pull into an underground garage of a hidden luxury bungalow with million dollar views of the bay. You could be forgiven for thinking the government was wasting money. And it does every day but not on this kind of real-estate. I'd be willing to bet this was seized from some organized crime lord, whose arrest was kept quiet so all the locals would continue to stay away. Meanwhile, anyone stationed here gets crap government-issued coffee while lounging in luxury.

The engine shuts off and without a word, we exit the car. I help Mia out, dropping a kiss on her temple. "Relax, sweetness. It's going to be okay," I say quietly in her ear.

She swipes a skeptical look my way, but her mouth softens. We walk to the interior stairs and head up.

The kitchen is as you might expect — what qualified as extremely high-end from about ten years ago. Since it was probably only used a handful of times while the kingpin owned it, it looks weirdly brand new. A couple of other government official types are sitting around with open laptops and cellphones. They look up to eye me with interest, and those expressions universally switch to frowns when they spot Mia.

"Gentlemen, this is my fiancée. She's not a part of any of this beyond what those idiots dragged her into yesterday, so treat her with respect. She's not to leave these premises without my say so and I'll be checking up on that every two hours at a minimum."

"Hold on, Price. You're not in charge of this…" he glances at Mia, "situation."

"No, but I am in control of my cooperation and if you want it, Mia stays."

They all show varying degrees of anger, annoyance, and amusement beneath the mask of stern calm that must be issued with a government badge. I know Mia would accuse me of doing the same, but it's never felt completely natural. And I can't wait to have time to scrub it off.

"Fine. Ma'am? Come with me, you can watch TV in the back room."

"What if I don't want to watch TV?" Mia sounds annoyed at his condescension.

"Then don't watch it but the volume has to stay up as you're not allowed to hear anything that's discussed here."

"Oh." She nods and follows him down the hall, giving me one wide-eyed glance over her shoulder.

"Boys? Let's get this over with."

There's no denying it's a long day. A doctor shows

up to give me a once over and take some blood to analyze. My guess is they won't find anything, but I'm happy enough to have them look. And I'd prefer the all clear before I fuck Mia again because contaminating her with something would be the proverbial nasty cherry on top.

It's also not too much longer before they realize they need Mia's input after all. One of the guys goes back to get her, and she follows him into the spacious living room, looking anxious. She relaxes when she sees me and hurries over to where I'm sitting on the couch. I waste no time pulling her down on my lap.

"Price? Seriously?" One of the agents scowls with disdain.

"Yes. Ask your questions fast so we can get out of here and your heart doesn't spasm with shock," I say dryly. "Mia? You know more than I do about what happened yesterday. They need to ask you some questions."

She nods while trying to edge off my lap, but I lock her down. I'm going to make damn sure everyone here knows that if they mess with her, they'll be facing my wrath.

Mia tells them everything she remembers and they manage to drag a few more details out of her that she hadn't thought to mention. They look a little shocked when she blithely tells them how fast she can hot wire a car. I'm tempted to have her show them, but that would just be petty. I do want to know where she learned to do that though, later. When they're done with all the questions, I lean down to give her a smacking kiss. "Proud of you, Mia."

She beams so brightly I'm ready to drag her into the nearest bedroom and show her just how proud I am. But not until I get the results of the damn blood test.

12

★ ★ ★

Mia

This whole thing is weird in ways I never could have previously imagined. When the unnamed man led me back to the rear bedroom, I was half-expecting an interrogation room with a little light torture. Instead, it's exactly as described — a bedroom with a large flat screen TV affixed to the wall. The whole place smells musty.

"What's your name?" I ask the man, who is busy fiddling with the remote.

"You can call me Steve," he replies absently, not looking up from the tiny buttons.

"Is that your code name or something?"

This time he looks up at me, his eyes laughing, which completely changes his face. "No. If I were going to pick a code name, it would be something much more exciting."

"Okay, Steve. You realize I don't want to watch TV, right?"

He shrugs. "Doesn't matter. Now, would you rather suffer through a game show, an action movie, or a telenovela?"

"Surely that thing has more than three channels."

"Yes, but those are guaranteed to be mostly noisy."

"Fine. Put on the telenovela then." I'm suspecting he's going to babysit me and this might get him hooked, making him suffer for months before he can break away from the storyline.

Or at least that's my idea. But instead he takes out his phone after he sets the channel on the TV and sits down in a chair by the door. Apparently he's completely engrossed in his messages. I sigh and go to the window to study the exterior surroundings. It's lush and tropical but otherwise completely nondescript with no clear landmarks. I sigh again. I wish I had my phone. I wish I was alone with Alexei, somewhere safe.

I start opening random drawers in the dresser and the nightstand, looking for something to occupy me because staring at the screen is not going to work with the way my nerves are on high alert. Occasionally Steve glances my way, rolls his eyes, and goes back to his phone. Eventually I land on a racy paperback with a swooning maiden on the front that looks like it's been in the drawer for at least thirty years. But there's something about smut that's pretty much timeless, so I take it over to the bed and fluff up the pillows. Maybe the seductive Lady Clare and her Norman lord will take my mind off things. It works for a chapter or two and then Steve's phone rings. He answers it without saying anything, which is really weird. Then he hangs up.

"Your turn, they have a few questions for you about yesterday." He stands and opens the door, waiting for me to precede him.

Fine. At least I can check on Alexei. I don't know much so their questions don't take too long and I can tell Steve is ready to take me back again, but I've got my own inquires to make. Alexei wasn't letting me get too far, so I don't exactly have to make an effort to get his attention from where I'm perched on his lap. "Did you see a doctor yet?"

"Yes, outwardly I'm all good. They're running the blood tests now." He looks tired, and I frown, rubbing my hand down his cheek. He half smiles into it. That does it. I turn back to the others, who aren't looking quite as intimidating as they were a few hours ago. "He needs to rest. And how much longer are you planning on keeping us here?"

There's a long silence like none of them think they owe me answers so nobody's going to jump to volunteer. Finally, the big one sighs. "He can rest when we're done, and that will be in another hour or so once we get the all clear signal. And no. I'm not telling you what that involves."

"Why not?"

"Because it's classified."

"I doubt it. You're just saying that to shut me up. Do you have the official levels of classification write-up? I know you have one or it can't be legally classified — so what category does telling me when I can leave fall into?"

I can feel Alexei's chest rocking with silent laughter behind me. I don't dare look at him.

"No. But trust me, we don't want to keep you here any longer than absolutely necessary." The man's voice is dry and I sniff.

"And where are you taking us at that point? I'm tired of fending off Russian goons. And I would like to eat a proper meal for once."

"This isn't a resort. We'll let you know when it's time."

"Fuck." Normally I don't let that kind of language fly except in private, but seriously?

They all ignore me, but I see one of them go in the kitchen and start opening drawers and cupboards. I rest my head down on Alexei's shoulder and try to be grateful that for the moment we're together and safe. Eventually a platter of sandwiches, constructed like they're feeding an army of workers, arrives on the table in the middle of the room. I sit up and take in Alexei, who's looking completely wiped.

"Okay, boys. I'm taking a plate of those and my man to the back room where he is going to rest. Got it?"

They glance at each other and shrug. One of the other men who has mostly stayed in the background speaks up, "Fine but no fucking unless you want us walking in — we'll be doing that anyway so don't do anything you don't want us watching."

I blush, because maybe a tiny part of me was thinking about snuggling. I tug Alexei to his feet and fill a paper plate with the best looking of the sandwiches. They're all heavy on the meat and light on veggies or cheese, but Alexei probably needs an extra burst of protein. He follows me down the hall and then we're both on the bed, leaning against the headboard. I don't bother shutting the door because if they're going to pop in to check they damn well better do it quietly.

Alexei stops eating after two sandwiches and stretches out next to me. I study his profile as he relaxes into sleep and will him silently to get better fast. Not that he hasn't made progress, but I want him back the way I found him. Maybe without the ugly shirt.

Mia

When I wake up, I'm alone in the bed. There's still a deep indentation in the fancy coverlet where Alexei was lying, but the room is quiet. The door to the adjacent bathroom is open and dark beyond. I don't think too much of it, after all I already discovered there's really nothing to do here. And it definitely feels like your grandma's second best guest room, the one that only gets vacuumed once a year because nobody ever goes in it.

I get up and use the facilities, splashing some cold water on my face to wipe the afternoon sleep lag off. It helps a little, but I'm still dragging. I guess it's all the excitement of the last couple of days. I head out to find Alexei, but I tense in the hallway. Something is different, something is really off. I sidle over to the wall and inch my way towards the open plan living room. I can't hear any rustling or conversation. Nothing. I mean, these guys were quiet from the get go but they were breathing. They made at least that much noise.

I peer around the corner and catch Steve's eye. He's leaning back in a chair, drinking a can of soda. He starts laughing. "What the hell are you doing?"

"Where is everyone? Where's Alexei?" My voice is sharp. I'm starting to panic.

Steve sobers and sits taller. "Take a seat."

"No. Where. Is. Alexei?"

"Would you sit down? I'm going to get a crick in my neck."

I snort. "Nice try, but you're still taller than I am. What have you done with Alexei?"

"Relax. Price is going to be fine."

"Going to be?" I screech. "What do you mean, 'going to be'?"

"He needed to go to the hospital for some further tests."

"Well, why didn't you wake me? I should be there with him."

"Mia." Steve uses my name for the first time. I sit abruptly.

"The hospitals in Hawaii aren't fully equipped for this kind of thing. He's in Washington."

I frown. Surely there's a hospital in Honolulu that can offer what you can get in Seattle. I say as much to Steve, who immediately shakes his head. "DC, Mia. Not Seattle. I honestly shouldn't be telling you even that much so I really can't say more."

"If you've locked him up in a secret government lab, I will cut off your balls and wear them as earrings." I glare at Steve, who unconsciously squeezes his thighs together. Men can be such babies about their junk. They all immediately cross their legs when anyone mentions taking a dog to be neutered. Try it, if you don't believe me.

"He's in a real hospital, Mia. I swear."

I humph. That's not really helping me get to him. "How can he be there already when he was here just a few hours ago?" I ask suspiciously. All of the things aren't adding up to my satisfaction.

"You've been asleep for six hours. Trust me, he's there already."

I frown again. It takes more than six hours to fly from Hawaii to DC. But then again, I doubt they took him commercial. "So you're here to take me to him, right?" My tone makes it clear there's only one acceptable answer, but Steve hesitates. "We can't do that. First, it's a secure government facility and second he's potentially contaminated."

"I thought you said it wasn't a secret government lab."

"It's not. It's a secure, military hospital. And lab." He smiles slightly at that.

"Well, if you think he's contaminated with what they gave him, wouldn't I be too?" I'm pushing the envelope of truth here a little too far and it's making me anxious, but I'm not leaving Alexei to be experimented on.

Steve's eyes widen with shock. "You mean you guys...?" This is it. The make or break moment and

I discover my moral line. I lie like a rug on the floor. "Yes. We exchanged bodily fluids. Several times, in all possible ways."

"Well, fuck."

Exactly, I think. He picks up his phone and sends a furiously typed text message. Then stares at the screen until it beeps with a reply.

"Looks like you just won yourself a free trip to DC. Come on. By the time we get to the base, the plane will be ready for us."

Well, it's not like I need to pack. And I hope karma forgives me the lie because it was all for a good cause. They'd better let me see Alexei or I will scream the walls down.

Sadly, when Steve pulls the cranberry sedan up to the waiting plane, it isn't some experimental supersonic jet. It's a rather boring aging mid-size jet, and it's full of military personnel who had been waiting around to board it. They just moved the scheduled departure time up an hour to accommodate us.

I'm too tense for the entire flight to enjoy either the view or the stories I'm overhearing. I'd be having a blast if I wasn't so worried. Or be drunk if it were a commercial flight but there's no drinks service here. Periodically I bombard Steve with questions to try to get a little more out of him. I do learn that Alexei was conscious when he left. Also that Steve broke up with his girlfriend six months ago because she said he traveled too much and never talked to her. Can't imagine where she came up with that one, poor girl (cue eye roll).

Thankfully, it's not another grandma sedan that meets us at the airport but a rather basic black mid-size car. Nondescript, clean, and sporting government license plates. But then half the cars in DC do, so it doesn't exactly stick out. We drive out through the suburbs. I've been to DC like twice in my life so I don't even recognize most things on a map let alone in person unless it's one of the monuments you see on TV. Certainly not the miles and miles of strip malls and concrete buildings that look like they're stuffed full of paper filing folders.

Steve's phone buzzes, it's' been doing that about every five minutes since we landed so I've started ignoring it. He never tells me who it is or what's going on, and he never seems too concerned. He glances my way with a small smirk. "You must be quite the girlfriend, Mia. Seems Price has turned uncooperative, so I'm to take you to his room first thing. Might give you a chance to get your stories straight."

I study him nervously. Does he know? I don't think so, he just suspects. And what are they going to do about it, anyway? "Good." I say stoutly.

Steve grins. "He's a lucky guy, Mia."

I smile with relief. I'm the lucky one. As long as I

get to stick by my man. Now I'm getting corny and pulling out sad country songs. That's what kind of day it's been.

13

★　★　★

Alexei

I swear someone is messing with my head, offering up Mia on a platter out of the blue, only to pull her away again. Now I'm half a world away and don't even know exactly where she is. All anyone will tell me is that she's safe. What the fuck does that mean? I'm not sure I can even trust them. Safe to them might mean grabbing her a hotel room in the seedy side of town and just leaving her there.

At the thought of that, my pulse picks up and I automatically swing my legs out of the hospital bed to go find her. Even though I've already been threatened with all sorts of bodily harm if I leave this hospital without clearance. I don't really give a damn.

Just then the door swings open, and Mia comes hurtling towards me. I grab her before she can fall to the floor. "Mia? How did you get here?"

She mumbles something into my chest, but I'm loathe to let her go, even enough to lift her head.

Every time I do, something bad happens. Mia seems to agree because she practically burrows into me, and it's then that I notice she's clutching me just as hard. Now I have to know.

"Baby? Did they treat you alright? What's wrong?"

She pulls back far enough to meet my gaze with a 'you seriously did not just ask that' expression. But then dives in with, "Alexei? What's wrong with you? Why are you in a hospital?"

I consider what to tell her. "They didn't recognize some of the compounds in my system. Mostly they're just making sure it's not anything that won't work it's way out eventually."

The man by the door that came in with Mia clears his throat like a threat. If I won't tell her, he will. I glare at him because obviously Mia's magic has worked on him as well, and now I have to make sure he doesn't try to steal her away.

"And… I might have collapsed again last night," I admit reluctantly.

Mia looks even more worried than she did when she walked in.

"I'm fine. Really." I hold her close against me, wondering if she's picked up on the fact that my cock is hard and pressed against her thigh. It has a completely automatic reaction whenever Mia's in the room.

Maybe she does notice because she turns back to the man. "Go away."

He smirks. "No."

"Who are you, again? Why are you still with Mia?"

"Did you want her to come on her own? On a troop carrier?" He looks disbelieving, but the smile in his eyes says he's enjoying this way too much. "And I'm Steve. Last name isn't pertinent to this op. Besides, Mia here says she might be contaminated." He leans back on the door with a grin, his arms folded over his chest.

Mia blushes, and my brain is putting two and two together.

"That's right," I say slowly, "and she could be pregnant. She's not to leave my side. Got it?"

"I'm not the one you need to convince, Price. But I do love a happy ending so try not to mess this up, yeah?"

The warning is clear. Cooperate and everything will work out. That's the company line and always has been, but it's also what got Mia into my mess, so... no.

"Family first," I respond flatly. It's a threat, and he knows it because the smirk disappears and his posture straightens.

"Fine, I'll go and find out status. Keep it clean,

kids. I'm not going to knock first." With a brief flick of his hand, he's out the door, and Mia is sagging against me.

"Seriously, Alexei. What's going on? Don't you dare die on me."

I can't hold back the kiss that I hope shows her that my dying isn't imminent. Not unless she decides she's had enough of my craziness and dumps my ass.

"Not going to die, love. They just want to drain all my blood so they can test the hell out of it. Freaking nurse is a sadist."

"I heard that." A cheery voice signals the incoming Nurse Hammond. Bane of my existence over the last twenty or so hours.

Mia bites her lip while the nurse draws yet more blood out of my arm. "Didn't you get enough the first time," she asks sharply.

The nurse blinks at her as if only just noticing her on my lap. "Well, at least you got him to sit still. The doc put in the order for the blood. I just do his dirty work." She smiles as she undoes the arm strap and takes off her gloves. "Bye-bye." And she's gone again.

"What the hell, Alexei?"

"I don't know, love. Honestly, the only thing I can tell you because it's all I know is I'm not radioactive.

The Geiger counter said so.”

She gasps in horror. I guess that hadn't occurred to her, but it's a definite risk factor when dealing with former Eastern bloc agents, official, rogue, or anything in between.

“Are they feeding you?”

“Yes. The food is crap, but there's plenty of it. Are you hungry?” I'm worried about her. She looks tired and drained. No surprise given the last few days, but she needs to rest and recuperate, maybe even more than I do. All in all, I'm feeling pretty good.

I pull her close to me again and pepper her with kisses until I see her smile starting to shine through her fatigue.

“Since I can't fuck you here, at least not properly, let's talk about our future together. Where you do want to live?”

“What are my choices?” She sounds uncertain, like I'm about to tell her she has to choose between three towns in rural Nebraska.

“Depends on whether you want to continue moving fish around or not, I guess. My military connections have been severed as of now.” Mia looks upset. “It was in the works anyway. This just shaved a couple of weeks off as I'm clearly more of a liability than an asset at this point. Beyond that, in theory I still have a job with ACI, although that was all part of the original deal. Maybe I'll stay home and be a kept man while you move the fish." I kiss the end of her nose, but she's still frowning. Not responding to my teasing, which worries me because she'd better not think I'd ever take a back seat to supporting my family. Not going to happen.

"So you'd come with me to Sala Bay while I figure that out?"

"If that's what you want, absolutely." My girl deserves to have everything she wants in life. Where we live is one of the easy ones, so why I wouldn't I let her pick?

Mia frowns harder, fiddling with the neckline of my stupid hospital gown. They stuck the damn thing on me while I was unconscious and stole my regular clothes, so it's this or go bare-ass naked. Practically the same thing based on the breeze up my back.

"I don't think you'll fit in my apartment."

I grin. "That's what you said about me before. Proved you wrong then, didn't I?"

She blushes furiously, and it's the cutest damn thing. I want to see if I can make her redder. "And if I'm buried balls deep in your pussy, that's a good nine inches of space free in your apartment."

Mia rolls her eyes rather than blushing. "Idiot. I just want to get us out of here before they think of some other reason to kidnap you."

"Me too. Maybe later today, okay? Last thing I want to do is make life harder on you if I'm not over whatever this shit is."

Mia

It's another two days before Alexei is allowed to leave the hospital. I didn't fight the powers that be on that, because he would have these sudden waves of weakness that would take hours to dissipate. He never blacked out though, and gradually they got farther apart and not as intense. They narrowed the substance down to some experimental nerve toxin from a South American toad that had been recently discovered. The toad wasn't new, but I guess nobody had tried using their slime for anything before. Gee, I wonder why?

You'd better believe I slept in the room with him. They brought in a cot for me after I made it clear I wasn't leaving for a hotel room. Not like I had a credit card on me, anyway. But even if I'd come with a month's worth of luggage, I wouldn't have left him. My ruse about being possibly contaminated mostly held up. They drew some blood, ran some tests, and told me I was fine. Nobody blinked when I told them I wasn't going anywhere without Alexei.

Only Alexei frowned because I wasn't sleeping in his bed, but I didn't see how he was going to get well if I spent the entire night on top of him cutting off his circulation. Because the bed just wasn't wide enough for two adults. Something he finally acknowledged for my sake when I pointed out I wasn't going to be able to sleep very well if I couldn't straighten my neck.

Now that we're walking out the front entrance, the world seems strangely paused. I haven't had my cell phone in days, I've no idea who, if anyone, has missed me, or is looking for me.

Someone has arranged for a driver to take us to the airport. Then the government is officially washing their hands of us, we're on our own from here on out. Other than the fact that we're thousands of miles away from where we started and they still don't have the bad guys in custody and maybe never will, I'm fine with it. The Russian goons are believed to have been recalled. That doesn't mean we won't encounter new goons, but Alexei says he's a much less attractive target now that he's officially logged out of all military networks. I still have no idea what he was doing in there, but there's not much point in asking because he's never going to tell me. And if he did, it would probably be all super high tech-speak, anyway.

What I'm most worried about right now is Alexei. Not his health, thank God, but he keeps giving me sideways glances and looking like he's about to say something. Then he doesn't. It happens at least ten times on the way to the airport, but I don't want to push him on it when there's a stranger within hearing distance. Just in case. I'm worried that he's decided I'm not the woman for him after all. Like maybe now that he's thinking clearly, he's realized he wants someone who will always be submissive to his bossy tendencies. And if that's the case, I'm not sure what to do about it.

He does it again when we're standing in front of the airline counter. "You sure about Sala Bay, Mia?"

I nod, confused. "All my stuff is there. We have to go back for that even if we head somewhere else later. Why?"

His eyes look slightly wary, but maybe that's my imagination because he doesn't hesitate to turn to the agent and say, "Two tickets to Seattle, please. Next available flight."

It's amazing how fast you can get on an airplane when you don't have any luggage at all, not even a carry-on. While we waited around in the hospital, we were able to get Alexei's wallet mailed in and we both got new cellphones and a new set of clothes. What I'd arrived in was such a mess I tossed it rather than try to revive it. It was an emergency outfit in the first place, so…

When we're seated in business class, something Alexei insisted on because of the length of his legs, I finally turn to him. "What's going on? You keep looking like you want to say something and it's scaring me a little. What aren't you telling me?"

He does that hesitation thing again, only now it's really obvious. "This isn't the time or place for this conversation, Mia."

Fuck. "Just tell me, Alexei. If you're breaking up with me, I don't want to wait five more hours to hear it. Just say it. I'm a big girl."

His eyes blaze with frustration. "Where the hell did you get that idea? You're more likely to tell me to get lost. Not like I'm much of an asset in your life."

"Why?" I'm practically nose to nose with him as we both make an effort to keep our voices down. I'm not sure it's working because I see a few surreptitious glances aimed our way.

"Because I didn't protect you, damn it."

I blink. Oh. This is an alpha male ego thing. For some reason, I didn't think Alexei had any insecurities. But of course he does. I frantically think of how to fix this. What can I say that will make him feel better about himself and not sound condescending?

"I started falling in love with you when you protected me from those assholes in Florida," I say cautiously, watching his face.

He waves a dismissive hand. "That wasn't life or death, I failed you when it really counted."

"Nooo," ah fuck, I hope I don't regret this. "Remember, you told me to jump off the dock? Several times and I refused. If I had, they wouldn't have come after me. So maybe you should punish me for not following orders." Like I ever would.

His green eyes gleam with relief as bright as the fasten seatbelt sign that's just illuminated over our heads. "That's right. I did tell you that." Something in his body relaxes, like he'd been tensed up and suddenly let go. "So tell me, sweet Mia, what kind of punishment would convince you to do as I say in the future?"

"Uhhh…" clearly I didn't think this through but I'm desperate here. Alexei's on a roll though. "Somehow I don't think reddening that sweet ass of yours will do it, do you?"

A spanking? Nobody has ever spanked me, not as a child and certainly not as an adult. The thought has me squirming in my seat for reasons I don't completely understand; the seatbelt digging into my hips.

"Err, probably not." I'm not sure where he's going with this, particularly given that we have a long flight ahead, but at least he doesn't look so depressed.

"Then I guess I'll have to think of something else." And with that he closes his eyes and leans back in the seat as the flight attendant starts going through the emergency notifications.

Now I'm the one that's nervous. What did I just open myself up for?

14

★ ★ ★

Alexei

I give myself a few minutes to indulge my fantasies. The dry air of the plane is already starting to irritate my sinuses, so I distract myself with images of Mia on her knees, eagerly sucking my cock. Her green-brown eyes sparkling with delight. Maybe I'd keep her naked for a week so I could watch her levels of arousal throughout the day. Tease her with brief touches, then pretend to walk away or say something naughty so she blushes all over. All this while trying to keep the smile off my face.

Teasing Mia is my new favorite hobby, although I didn't miss her flicker of interest when I threatened to spank her. Something we can explore when she's ready and everything has calmed down. I don't actually want or need her to follow my commands blindly. That might be fun for a few minutes, but my real life concern here is that she's not putting her safety first. That has got to be her top priority at all times because it sure as fuck is mine.

How I convince her to adopt a new attitude about that is a challenge. I'll come up with something. Meanwhile, it feels good to let her fuss, just a little.

"Alexei?" Her voice suggests she might be on to what I'm picturing on the backs of my eyelids so I open them reluctantly. Her hazel eyes are watching me with suspicion. I wait for her to say what's on her mind.

"You told those government clones I was your fiancée."

I nod affirmatively, confused as to where this is going. We've talked about our future together.

"You never actually asked me. Or even said it directly to *me*."

I frown. Sure I did. When… Okay, maybe I didn't. "Won't that feel a little fake if I ask you now?" I ask her, eyeing the narrowness of the aisle. I've got my doubts that if I tried to get down on one knee, I'd ever get up again.

"Right this minute, yes. It would. But that doesn't let you off the hook. I don't want you taking me for granted." She's biting her lip again. Fuck.

"Mia, sweetness. That's exactly the point I've been trying to make. I don't take you for granted because you are the most precious thing in my life. I want you to see yourself the same way. So when I say jump, you jump and keep that sweet ass safe so I know you're somewhere I can find my way back to. Can't do that if you're dead."

"Oh." Silent tears are leaking out of the corners of her eyes, making them glisten. I brush them away with my thumb and lean down for a soft kiss. Then I can't help myself from whispering in her ear, "So you'll marry me, right? So I can spank you when you forget how precious you are?"

Her gurgling chuckle lights my heart. "We might need an edited version of that to tell the grandchildren. And I thought we just agreed you weren't asking now?"

"Kitten, I do not schedule marriage proposals on my calendar. It's either right or it isn't. And before you get too caught up in where your mind just went, you are the only woman I've ever proposed to. You wouldn't want to scar my psyche by saying no."

Her smile broadens. "No, I wouldn't want to do that. I guess I'll have to marry you then."

"Don't sound so excited." I kiss her again to seal the deal. She unbuckles her seatbelt so she can lean into me more easily, and I hold her there.

"It's better than all my fantasies, Alexei," she mumbles.

Wait. "What fantasies, Mia? I want to hear them all. Now. With details. That's an order."

She laughs again and nestles into my side.

I sigh at her refusal. "Fine. Then tell me how you know how to hot wire a car? I hate to be judgmental but you don't seem the type."

She giggles softly into my shoulder. "It was one of those adult education classes to teach women how to deal with basic car repairs on their own. It wasn't technically part of the curriculum but the instructor showed us, so we'd know what was involved. I think he was trying to make a point about locking up. Anyway, he let us try it on the junker car we were using for class. I was just really good at it, like immediately. I have no idea why and I've never used it since outside of that classroom until this week."

"Any other hidden talents I should know about?"

She rolls her eyes at me. "Like I'm going to tell you that before the wedding? Pfft." She blows her hair out of her face in mock annoyance. I know to the marrow of my bones I'm never going to be bored living with Mia. I can't fucking wait.

Mia

My apartment shrank while I was gone. Like a lot. Or maybe it's just because Alexei is huge, even though he can move without making a sound. When we arrived straight from the airport we did nothing more exciting than order pizza to be delivered and fall into bed. Both of us too tired to do more than sleep.

And the first half of the day has been taken up with answering frantic emails, canceling credit cards and all the stuff that goes along with having Russian agents steal your purse. I wouldn't worry so much if they'd taken it with them, but my guess is they dumped it so who knows where all that stuff is now. Sarah was of course frantic based on the emails in my inbox, but I had to leave her a voicemail. Likely she's out in the jungle somewhere and we'll have to catch up later.

Alexei, whose wallet is intact and doesn't have to listen to annoying hold music for hours on end, is busy figuring out how and when to get us legally married. I wouldn't have put that as a day one priority, but there was no moving him on the subject and at least it keeps him seated at my kitchen table out of the way.

We are going to need to figure out where we want to live long term really soon. I wish he had a stronger opinion about that and whether he wants to continue working at Alpha Corps, but he insists he'll adapt to whatever I decide.

Now that we're both safe, I have to admit I had some fun being a spy, even if it didn't have anything to do with the war games, really. And I surprised myself with how well I did, thinking on my feet. Maybe that had something to do with the need to rescue Alexei, but there's a part of me that wants to try it again. But then I think that might give my future husband a heart attack. Sooo… I'm just not sure.

Jobs aside, if I could pick any place in the world to live it would be on an island. One big enough to have some basic services like a doctor and a grocery store but not so big that it has bridges everywhere. Maybe when Alexei is done researching, I'll do some of my own.

As if he heard my thoughts, he snaps my laptop shut and stands up. "You about done over there?"

"For the moment." I cross the last item off of my emergency list — getting my driver's license reissued. 8-10 days in the mail, they said. Great.

"Then you and I have some unfinished business, kitten."

Startled, I look up from my notes to see him pointing firmly towards the bedroom.

"Um, Alexei?"

"Now, Mia." His voice is stern, but his eyes are gleaming. A flutter of excitement starts in my belly. Slowly, I stand up from my small desk and walk over to him. He spins me by my shoulders and gives me a gentle push. "Naked and on the bed, Mia. By the time I get in there or there will be consequences."

Oooh, my panties are starting to steam, I think. I don't know why I find this side of him so enticing, but I do. I'm not sure I'm ready for what he has in mind, though. I glance uncertainly over my shoulder as I pause at the doorway. He gives me a wicked smirk and I relax. Alexei is never going to go anywhere I'm not ready for. And I'm thrilled to have the bossy Alexei back in rotation. In moderation, of course.

I strip and think about how I want him to find me. He didn't say, so he must be leaving this part up to me. Flat on my back just seems so obvious and I'm no gymnast so in the end I lie on my front facing the door so I can watch him when he comes in. I'm lying on top of my favorite pink patchwork quilt and it occurs to me I have no idea of the etiquette for this sort of thing. Are you supposed to pull the quilts back? Or just expect to wash everything on a daily basis? Obviously hotel rooms are a different story, but maybe I should have…?

Alexei comes in less than a minute after I got undressed. He grins when he sees me watching him, my eyes just about level with his impressive bulge.

"I believe I owe you a serious fucking, young lady. And it's several days overdue so there will be interest."

"There will?" I squeak. I mean, how much more can he add on? Or do I even want to know?

"Absolutely. I always pay my debts." He strips efficiently and my mouth goes dry at the sight of his impressive cock, ready and eager for me. I lick my lips and Alexei groans. "Not now, kitten. This time is all about you."

I start to sit up, but he stops me with a gentle but firm hand on my spine. "No. You picked this position, and this is where you're going to stay."

Oh. I gulp. Because once he moves from directly in front of me, I'm staring at myself in the mirror over my dresser. How did I not notice that before?

Alexei pulls me up slightly at my hips and slips a pillow under and then straddles me from behind. I watch all this in the reflection, my pussy aching and wet as he leans down and slowly kisses up my spine, lingering for what feels like hours at the juncture of my neck and shoulder. He nips the top curve of my ear and my pussy throbs in response. His dark head looks even more black against the medium brown of my hair as I watch what I can't feel and feel what I can't see.

I'm groaning audibly when he finally scoots backwards and adds another pillow under my hips. The dent in his chin somehow looks extra deep in the reflection. His hands part my ass cheeks and he blows gently on my hot folds. I gurgle, "Gah!" is all I can manage. Alexei's chuckle is pleased and I lower my head to the bed when he starts licking my pussy from my clit down. I spasm hard and fast when he bites down gently, my legs quaking under his thighs. "Alexei!"

"Hmmm?"

"Stop torturing me. Just fuck me already."

"Mia, you seem to have gotten the wrong idea. I believe I promised to fuck you until I was dry. Nothing in that statement should give you the impression that this is going to go fast or be over with anytime soon. So I suggest you relax."

"Fuck!" I groan into my folded arms. He laughs, and that's when I feel the head of his thick cock nudge my entrance. He pulls my hips up slightly for a better angle and then he slides home in one long slow stroke. I hadn't realized I was holding my breath until I let it out in a sigh of deep satisfaction.

He feels so good. I want to hang onto this moment and frame it. That's when I bring my head up to look in the mirror again. Alexei's green eyes meet mine in the reflection and he holds my gaze as he pulls out and drives back in. His eyes are wild and they grow hotter as I push my hips back, meeting his thrusts with my own. Each stroke hits that magic spot, and I can feel my climax building again. But I'm ignoring that. Mostly. I'm watching for his. I need to see him lose control, to lose himself in my body and really let go.

I get my wish. Just as the tremors of another orgasm start to ripple outwards, Alexei pounds into me with a furious rhythm before leaning his head back with a roar. I feel long ropes of his cum pulse into me as I watch his chest heave as if he's gasping for air. Then he's down over me. Bracing his weight on his arms on either side of my head, his cock still throbbing deep inside me. I lean slightly to kiss his arm, the only part of him I can reach in this position and the change in angle sends a fresh spurt of cum deep into my channel. Alexei groans as if I really did wring him dry.

"Kitten. Give me a sec," he rasps into my ear.

I'm content to feel him, in me, all around me, in this little apartment where I used to daydream of this very moment, even when I couldn't quite imagine the details. I tighten my internal muscles around him in a subtle warning not to dispel the magic too quickly. He groans again with a half-laugh. And finally, *finally*, says something in Russian before dropping a kiss on my shoulder blade.

I haven't got a freaking clue what he just said.

Epilogue

★   ★   ★

Alexei

One year later

I'm standing on the low bluff overlooking Honeysuckle Bay, frowning as I watch my wife scan the pebble shore for shells and sea glass. She shouldn't be out in this wind, not in her condition. The problem is, I can't call her back in without letting on that I know, and I really don't want to spoil her surprise. Not if I don't have to. So I'm watching her every move like a hawk, ready to swoop in and carry her away to safety at the slightest hint of danger. Mostly she just rolls her eyes at me and keeps doing whatever it was she was doing that made me nervous.

I want her to be the one to tell me she's pregnant. I've known for about three weeks. You can't make love to your wife on a daily basis and not know when her breasts are fuller, more tender or, sadly, when she can't take your cock in her mouth even slightly without gagging. A small price to pay, given how long

I've wanted to see her belly round with my child. It's not logical, but it's a deep primal instinct that says a baby makes everything permanent. A forever link between us. I need her to tell me.

Thank fuck she at least took herself to the doctor last week. But she only smiled when I asked her and said it was 'routine'. And when I swung by Dr. Mason's clinic on my way back from the hardware store, I practically growled in frustration when he wouldn't tell me anything. He at least relented sufficiently to tell me she was fine. Which, according to him, was already crossing a line regarding privacy. I sigh, watching her bend to pick up something interesting from the beach, turning it over and over between her fingers before slipping it into her bag with a smile.

Mia makes her way slowly up the beach towards where I'm standing, pushing her curls out of her face as she turns away from the wind. She's glowing, and I greet her with a deep kiss when she joins me.

"Mia…" I can't take it anymore.

"Alexei, love, you've lasted way longer than I thought you would. Yes, you knocked me up. Yes, everything is fine and I hope you've learned a lesson."

"You were testing me?" I mock growl in her ear as I hold her close against me, my arms locked around her.

"Nooo, trying to train you, maybe. You did pretty well

the last few weeks, keeping the overprotectiveness mostly in check. Notice I said mostly, you're still pretty bad."

I'm frowning again. "Baby..."

"No. Alexei, the baby, not just me, needs me to live a normal, healthy life. Unless or until a *doctor* says otherwise. That's why I didn't tell you right away so you could see that everything's going fine without me sitting around all day."

She hugs me tight. "I wanted to, you know, as soon as I knew. But you knew already didn't you?"

I nod jerkily. "Probably. Your body started changing, your appetite is different too."

"God, I know it. I'm freaking starving."

"Then let's go feed you." I start to drag her towards the house, but she stops me with a laugh.

"This, Alexei, that's what I don't need. Don't get me wrong, it's sweet, but I don't need to be smothered. I can make myself a sandwich when I'm ready."

"Tell me you're at least going to cut back on work?"

Now she's frowning. "We'll see. The new manager is making things difficult. Sarah offered me a job with the war games people, taking over part of her role. The part that can be done remotely. She's cutting back on her hours too now that they have a kid."

"Remotely." I chew over that word. "So no flirting."

She goes up on her tiptoes to kiss my cheek. "Only with you, Alexei, and no spying either, and no Russian goons." She adds as an afterthought.

We walk back to our house, an old 1930s farmhouse we purchased directly from ACI, along with the five acres of land that surround it when we took over as caretakers of the Embrace Island facility. It took some hard negotiating, but we weren't going to invest our money and muscle into renovating a house we didn't own. ACI had no problem with that once they realized it meant we were much less likely to move off the island in six months like the last five people in the job.

The facility isn't used for much these days. It was an old airbase back when people were worried about the Japanese invading but once that was over the Army decided it didn't need it anymore. So they sold it off to Alpha Corps, which grabbed it for a song because nobody knew the west coast was going to blow up in population and popularity. Mostly ACI just sits on it protectively like a dragon with a hoard. But they need someone out here to make sure trespassers don't cause any trouble and occasionally to give a tour to some exec that spots it on an asset list and wants to know more.

Island living is different, but it suits us. For one, it's a lot harder for any strangers to sneak onto the island without being noticed. They instantly stand out like a sore thumb, especially in winter. So while I know Mia is aware that the Russians coming back is extremely low probability, she feels better here than in the city. And whatever makes Mia happy… except when she overdoes things.

Mia

3 years later

"Alexei!" I shout from the back door, not sure where he and our twin toddler daughters have gotten to.

"We're coming," he calls back and I wait impatiently, bouncing on the balls of my feet over the email I just received from Sarah.

Two small human spheres wearing matching red jackets gyrate up the path to the house. I don't know why it is that little kids can't move in a straight line. Or maybe they just don't want to. Either way, it's funny as heck. Eventually the girls reach me, each giving one of my legs a hug like they've been gone for days. It's been maybe forty-five minutes. I help them off with their jackets, shaking my head over their absolute insistence, before they could even talk, that critical items like coats and shoes had to match. Amazing what two toddlers crying in a store will get a mom to do. Yeah, I didn't stand a chance. Matching jackets is not the hill to die on.

Alexei brings up the rear and leans in for a kiss. His lips are warm but his face is wind chilled. I finger that cleft in his chin that still has me going weak in the knees. He cocks an eyebrow of inquiry.

"The war games are going to be here this year."

"You're f…" he catches himself just in time, "kidding me?" he concludes lamely, rolling his eyes at Amelie and Geneva, who are watching us like hawks.

I shake my head with a grin. "Nope, apparently everything is in the works for July, starting with a celebratory 4th of July company party, moving into the war games and then some other stuff they have planned. They're talking two months in total. They'll be sending out an advance team to do the logistics for the tents and electricity, all that kind of jazz. Isn't it cool?"

Alexei is frowning slightly. "Maybe. You're not thinking about trying out spying again, are you?"

"No, love. I'm a little past that phase of life, don't you think?"

"We going to have to revisit that lesson on just how precious you are, kitten?"

I swallow hard. Even with two small kids around, Alexei can have me wet and wanting in seconds. He always finds some way to make sure I don't have to suffer for very long, even if it involves calling in a favor from our nearest neighbor to watch the kids. Sascha never asks why, she just grins and leads the girls away. I blush, Alexei smirks, and the world keeps turning.

He taps my butt in warning. He's still never delivered on the threatened spanking, but he likes to bring it up now and then. I think he knows the idea gets my imagination going. And a few other things…

"Ha, just so you know, I'm determined to find Sascha the perfect guy, and this might be a golden opportunity. So don't count on having your emergency babysitter forever."

"For that, you're going to have to wait until after dinner."

I pout, although not really seriously. After dinner will be fine, the girls look worn out from playing on the beach, hopefully they'll be fast asleep right after bath time.

I have my own ways of returning the torture, though. I lean in to kiss him and say softly, "So I was thinking this might be a good time to have another one." I cast a meaningful glance down at the two dark heads dancing around us. They got their daddy's hair, lucky ducks. Alexei's eyes start doing that weird glow thing they do when he's clamping down on his control.

"I'll take care of bath time and the story tonight. You just get ready for me. Turn the heat up too, make it like Hawaii if you want, because you're going to be too busy to get under the covers for quite a while, kitten. I don't want you getting cold."

With Alexei, it comes out sounding like both a threat and a promise. Probably why a shiver of delight scoots down my spine and starts my clit throbbing. I sigh with happiness as I turn towards the kitchen to start dinner. It's a lucky woman who can say her husband is better than all of her previous fantasies. *Combined.*

Preview
Challenging Burke

1

★ ★ ★

Cassidy

I know I've got a serious geeky side although I never thought I'd cream my panties over a piece of tech. But that little drone is *fine*. As soon as they call for volunteers, I'm not only raising my hand, but I stand up and walk to the podium. Up close it's even more impressive. It's a true micro drone, not compromising on any of the bells and whistles. It's got a full HDR video stream, audio, night vision and it fits in the palm of my hand. Who wouldn't want to play with that?

There are some grins and giggles behind me, but not from the woman with the microphone who is wearing a peach suit that is vastly inappropriate for the muddy environment, matching heels, and a concerned expression. "Are you sure, um," she glances down at my nametag, "Cassidy? This might be a great opportunity for you to break through some barriers?" She really says that last bit as if she knows me personally and thinks I'm shy.

I'm perplexed for a minute, wondering if she's confused me with someone else before it hits me. Oh, my face. I'm so over other people somehow thinking it's all new to me. "No, I want that drone." I look her straight in the eye and dare her to challenge me on it further. Her gaze drops, and she steps back.

And I do want it. I have serious plans for that little baby, not all of them on the up and up. But HR lady who's determined to make me feel like a victim of society or genetics or something doesn't need to know that. A few other women who weren't quite so bold come up when they're called after raising their hands and join me. They look nervous and excited — I think this might be pushing at their comfort boundaries already, but I can't wait to get started. My older brothers are going to be so jealous when I tell them. Hopefully, all the details aren't classified because that would be a real bummer. It's rare that I have better stories to tell than they do. I don't want to miss my chance at the next family get together.

Another woman comes up and hands each of us a few sheets of paper with basic instructions on where to go and what our mission will be. Then she takes our names and tent assignments. All told it's a group of five that become the mini drone squad. We start training in the morning.

Once that's squared away, I return to my uncomfortable gray metal folding chair at the back of the tent and let the rest of the presentation roll over me. My role for the next two weeks has been determined so I don't feel a great need to pay attention to how to seduce a man the HR-approved way. Which quite frankly sounds ridiculous and like something out of a 1950s video about being an 'asset' as a decorative secretary. No touching, no nudity, but batting eyelashes is fine. Blah, blah, blah.

The woman next to me mutters "fucking idiots" under her breath. I turn to her with a grin that she returns with an embarrassed whisper, "Sorry!"

I turn back so I'm facing forward but whisper to her out of the corner of my mouth, "Do you think anyone follows these stupid rules?"

She snorts softly. "Maybe that woman up there in the front row, the one with the ruffles."

My eyes trail along the row of chairs far in front of us to see who she's talking about. Oh. Her. There's a woman of indeterminate age, at least from the back, whose street clothes consist of what looks like a pink and green ruffled pinafore. Her dark hair is in some kind of fancy braided up do. "Probably a stripper," I whisper back to my neighbor, who giggles loudly before slapping a hand over her mouth.

"I'm Violet, by the way," she says softly when she regains control.

"Cassidy," I respond back.

"Want to get lunch together? I'm not sure I can

take much more political correctness."

"Sure. Is it coming soon?"

I can hear the smile in her voice. "The schedule says fifteen minutes."

Well, they have been keeping to a schedule like it really is the military. Which it isn't, but try telling that to any of the testosterone jocks employed by ACI.

The lady doing the talking starts going faster as if she can see a countdown clock and has to get through all her words before then. Her razor-cut blonde bob swings with her fierce enthusiasm over personal growth. And maybe she can see a clock because there's a soft gong and suddenly everyone is on their feet, heading to the aisles as if they were poised on the edge of their seats, just waiting for the signal. I exchange a look with Violet who now that we're standing is about a half a foot shorter than me and cute as a button. I'll bet she hates that. Her dark hair is making perfect corkscrew curls. I have no idea if it's always that way or just doing something special because of the humidity. Already I've noticed my own hair has taken on a life of its own. I've yet to decide if that's a good thing.

It's just starting to rain outside, big swaths of mist moving between the large evergreens on the edge of the compound. I can't wait to explore the woods here because I hear there are no poisonous critters to watch out for, but I have yet to set foot in them. I guess you can't have trees growing up right against the runway.

We follow the crowd to the big mess hall, which is in another giant tent two down from where we were being held in HR purgatory. And wouldn't you know it, all those military guys got there first. They already have filled most of the cafeteria tables, and the last few men are making their way through the lines.

"Fuckers," I mutter. I'll bet they knew when we would be arriving and timed the end of their presentations to finish five minutes earlier. We'll be lucky if there's any food left.

There is, but it's mostly 'girl food' as in salads and fruit smoothies. Violet and I exchange eye rolls before filling our trays with what we can find and claiming one of the tables that's already being vacated by big, tough men dressed in green camo. I eye their retreating backs, wondering if any of them are about to report to me.

That's part of my personal secret mission. I've been given a promotion. Only just last week and it's not been made public yet. And I'm scared out of my ever-loving mind because not only am I five years younger than the youngest person on my new team but they're all combat veterans. I don't talk that talk and I definitely don't walk the walk. But now I'm their boss, well I will be in three weeks' time. And three of the five men are here at the war games somewhere. I know their names and I've read their files, but I don't know their assignments here. I'm hoping I can figure that out tonight when they post all the 'meet your teammates' stuff that they've promised. Then I'm going to do a little spying that has nothing to do with the games' objective of capturing Airstrip #1. All the big tents are pitched on the tarmac of Airstrip #2 so at least that won't be a point of confusion. I hope. Some of these guys look tough but like maybe they don't have that much processing capacity. I want to get a sense of the men reporting to me before they know I'm watching, so I have some idea of what I'm up against. I know I can't be their buddy, but I'd like it if it didn't have to be all out war. And it shouldn't be. I mean, I want them to succeed and I want to succeed too. Shouldn't be in conflict, right?

Burke

Getting old sucks. It's not the number, or even the subtle creaking in my knees, it's my damn response time going down by whole seconds. Even when I work out an extra hour a day and feel fitter than I ever have. The clock doesn't lie. And the time on the clock says I'm no longer the fastest rescue swimmer in or out of the Navy. Not by a lot. And I'm starting to feel the cold in ways I didn't ten years ago.

I know what that means, my support staff know what that means. Retirement to another job or the dreaded coaching position held by so many former champions. I haven't decided which one I hate least but I've got about two weeks to make up my mind. Because while I might be able to continue rescue swimming in low-risk environments like this one, where it's unlikely anything serious is going to happen, the days of high seas adventures are clearly over. Part of me says fine, let the next generation suck in too much salt water and bang sharks on the nose. And another part of me rails against fate, mostly because nothing more exciting has come along to lure me into my forties with enthusiasm.

I'm bored.

It doesn't help that I've got this little two-person tent by the water's edge to myself. Pablo, the other swimmer who's supposed to relieve me on duty, having decided that this tent is much too far away from the female contingent, has removed himself to the big barracks. He won't get any sleep but can leer at girls over breakfast first thing. Or something. If he thinks he's getting any, he hasn't figured out that the women are also in group tents and don't have any privacy. Or maybe that doesn't bother him. I don't care enough to find out.

I'm stretched out on my narrow cot, staring up at the khaki fabric ceiling, wondering how long before the rain pounding on it starts to seep through. No sign of it yet, but I don't see canvas winning the battle against Mother Nature. At this point, this is the most exciting thing I have to look forward to.

A high-pitched buzzing catches my attention and

my first thought is a mosquito, because what else could add more pain and irritation to the day now that it's almost over? But when I glance around, trying to track the microscopic motherfucker, I see a drone instead.

It's tiny. I didn't even know drones came that small — about the size of a small apple, complete with a blinking red eye and four little rotors. I watch it move across the tent towards the stack of reading material I was given. Not all my reflexes are gone to shit because I'm able to upend a water glass over it with minimal effort. The glass was empty, so I doubt any damage was done to the drone. Now I can take my time figuring out who the fuck is spying on me and why.

I mean I know this is a war games but I'm here purely in a support capacity in case of emergency, not part of the assigned feuding sides. Which means I should be about as boring as it can get to anyone looking for intel. Maybe the little drone is just lost. Except as Pablo pointed out multiple times, this tent really is a long way away from everything else. Huh.

The little drone is hopping and buzzing, trying to shift the glass off the stack of books through sheer force of will. It makes me smile watching it. The glass is heavy, and the drone isn't. Eventually it settles down as if waiting for something, and I eye it cautiously. I want to examine it more closely, but not at the expense of having it fly away. I'll check it in the morning. Surely those things have batteries that will wear down by then?

I'm feeling more energetic now just having something new to think about, so I decide to change into running clothes and head out for a jog on the beach. I'm used to running in the rain. If anything, it's invigorating, and it tends to keep everyone else out of my way. I'm committed to this plan until I strip down. With my pants down around my knees I'm startled by the furious buzzing of the tiny drone. It whirrs back to life and turns around, its red light blinking furiously at the wall.

For the first time in forever, I laugh so hard I have to sit down. Who knew drones could be embarrassed by human nudity? And honestly, I've spent so much of my life parading around in nothing more than a tiny lycra bathing suit that I don't think too much of it with humans either. I mean, I usually remember to put on more clothes to go to the grocery store, but not always. They fucking mean that no shirt, no service thing, so I've had to resort to keeping spares in my car because I'm always forgetting when I live in a warmer climate.

So this little dot of tech practically blushing is fucking hilarious. And it means only one thing. There's a girl on the other end of it, I'd bet my life on it. And now my interest in jogging has flown out the window and I want to know more about her and why she's flown a micro drone into my tent. I mean,

I *really* want to know. I snag a pair of sleep pants that I brought thinking it might be cold here and pull them on. I've no idea if the drone has audio but I'll bet it does so I say as gently as I can, "You can turn around now. I'm decent."

There's a long pause and then it slowly and almost reluctantly rotates back 180 degrees. The rotors are still spinning, but I ignore that and sit back down on my cot. Time to do a little research into all the propaganda they send out for these things.

It takes ten minutes but I finally find it. And I'm quirking an eyebrow at the drone while staring at it. It's not moving, but I feel like it's watching me. I glance down at the paperwork again. According to this, any drone operator who loses physical control of his or her drone for twenty-four consecutive hours is declared 'dead'. The same as if they were shot by one of the paintball guns. My drone girl is in some serious shit. And I'll bet my cozy little tent that she'll be by sometime later tonight to try to repatriate her equipment. Which means if I want to get a good look at her and find out her name, I've got some work to do.

"Sorry, sweetheart," I say cheerfully as I drop a towel over the glass-covered drone and then I move it and the stack of books over into the far corner. Next I reposition the cots so that the only way to the drone is over my bed. And I double check the back walls to make sure there's no easy point of entry under them either. Just to be safe, I put a box over the drone ensemble and pile some more shit on top.

Now for the girl. I've no idea what size she might be, but it's highly unlikely I can't take her. But I don't have anything to restrain her with, like handcuffs, and I doubt very much she'll be in the mood to sit and chat. I eye my jacket and assorted other crap lying around. I'm not exactly neat - and don't believe what those recruitment posters tell anxious mothers. Yeah, I used to get in trouble on a regular basis for my mess, but that never made me any neater. I suppose I could smother her in clothes, tie the arms together or something. I don't want to hurt her, so sitting on her seems like not a great idea.

It would really help if I had some idea of who she is. I flip back through all the materials and even look online. But there are too many people and no mention of drones. Must have been something that was doled out on site. Guess I'll just have to be patient for a few more hours.

— Find out what happens next in Challenging Burke, Book 2 of ACI Unleashed

Thank you for reading!

Get another peek into the world of ACI with Lucy (Sarah's sister-in-law) who has her own adventure with a modern day Viking/Swedish Special Forces soldier. Get her story when you sign up for my newsletter.

https://BookHip.com/ZNBSVAS

About Me

I write lighthearted steamy romance featuring alphalicious heroes who know what they want and strong, smart heroines that can spot gold underneath a tough exterior.

My promise to you: no cheating, always an HEA, and more than a few silly bits.

I love my characters and I want them all to live happily ever after (along with fabulous careers, chubby babies, and/or adorable pets.) Sometimes this requires letting go of how the real world works. I'm okay with that and I hope you are too!

I live and work in the wilds of the Pacific Northwest where I like to experiment with making wine and sourdough bread when I'm not writing or being lectured by my adorably entitled chickens.

Looking For More?

Grab this printable reading list that has what's out, what's coming, and what formats are available.

https://tinyurl.com/OliviaBooks

That presumes I've updated it! And if you think I might have forgotten or even to just say hi, you can reach me at: oliviasinclairbooks@gmail.com. I love hearing from readers and I do my best to respond to everyone.